KT-599-610

Renew by phone or a

LIBRARY SERVICES
WITHDRAWN AND OFFERED FOR SALE
SOLD AS SEEN

1804671827

SPECIAL MESSAGE TO READERS

THE ULVERSCROFT FOUNDATION
(registered UK charity number 264873)
was established in 1972 to provide funds for
research, diagnosis and treatment of eye diseases.
Examples of major projects funded by
the Ulverscroft Foundation are:-

- The Children's Eye Unit at Moorfields Eye Hospital, London
- The Ulverscroft Children's Eye Unit at Great Ormond Street Hospital for Sick Children
- Funding research into eye diseases and treatment at the Department of Ophthalmology, University of Leicester
- The Ulverscroft Vision Research Group, Institute of Child Health
- Twin operating theatres at the Western Ophthalmic Hospital, London
- The Chair of Ophthalmology at the Royal Australian College of Ophthalmologists

You can help further the work of the Foundation
by making a donation or leaving a legacy.
Every contribution is gratefully received. If you
would like to help support the Foundation or
require further information, please contact:

THE ULVERSCROFT FOUNDATION
The Green, Bradgate Road, Anstey
Leicester LE7 7FU, England
Tel: (0116) 236 4325

website: www.foundation.ulverscroft.com

SKYHORSE

Judge Nathan Berkley requests a seemingly simple task of his adopted son, Appaloosa King: ride to the remote town of Deadlock to pick up Catherine, the judge's newly-discovered daughter. Trouble starts when, on the way, King leads his two cowboys off on a diversion, aiming to meet up with a mysterious messenger — who, unbeknownst to the trio, has a deadly reason for the rendezvous. All looks lost until a stranger arrives on the scene — the man known as Skyhorse . . .

Books by John Ladd
in the Linford Western Library:

SMOKING BARRELS

JOHN LADD

◆

SKYHORSE

Complete and Unabridged

LINFORD
Leicester

First published in Great Britain in 2014 by
Robert Hale Limited
London

First Linford Edition
published 2015
by arrangement with
Robert Hale Limited
London

Copyright © 2014 by John Ladd
All rights reserved

A catalogue record for this book is available
from the British Library.

ISBN 978–1–4448–2501–5

Published by
F. A. Thorpe (Publishing)
Anstey, Leicestershire

Set by Words & Graphics Ltd.
Anstey, Leicestershire
Printed and bound in Great Britain by
T. J. International Ltd., Padstow, Cornwall

This book is printed on acid-free paper

Dedicated to Johnny Depp

Prologue

The forest was dense. Somewhere within its uncharted boundaries Kiowa and Cheyenne tolerated one another but frowned upon all unexpected visitors to what was to become known as Indian Territory. There was a trail that dared to cross the land from east to west, but to travel along it was perilous and often fatal.

Stagecoaches ventured through the forested terrain but to try and avoid attack they varied the days and times when they crossed the dangerous land. There were fewer and fewer places where the nomadic tribes were allowed to exist any longer.

The stagecoach companies had to honour their contracts with the US Mail, and that meant they had to run the risk of losing the lives not only of their drivers and guards but also those

of their passengers. A newly con-
structed railroad ran to the north of the
forest and slowly but surely was
bringing about the end of the once
all-powerful stagecoach giants.

The Overland Stagecoach company
had seen its monopoly of the major
links between the largest of towns and
cities disappear and had been forced to
take on the smaller routes between towns
where the locomotives could not reach.

Few if any lone riders ever ventured
into the forest and survived to tell the
tale. If they had to travel through
Indian Territory they tended to go by
stagecoach, in which they had the
added safety of other well-armed
passengers as well as a skilled shotgun
guard to protect them.

As with all routes employed by the
stagecoach companies the need for way
stations was vital. These were places for
weary passengers to rest up and have a
meal whilst a fresh team of horses were
guided between the traces of the
vehicle. The small town of Poisoned

Springs was such a settlement, set two miles from the forest.

It consisted of a dozen buildings, and half of those were abandoned. Only those close to the way station building remained occupied by stagecoach workers. It was more akin to an old-style trading post than a standard way station and although its main purpose was to cater for the company's passengers it also traded with the Indians, who knew that in exchange for fur pelts they could get things that were otherwise prohibited.

Whiskey was the remote station's most profitable and popular of provisions. Guns and ammunition were also illegally traded for the valuable fur pelts.

As with many remote places on the very edge of civilization the law rarely visited. There were fortunes still to be made and always a certain type of men willing to risk all to make them.

The manager was as wide as he was tall. His name was Olin Thorson and he would sell his own mother if the price was right. If he had ever had any scruples they had disappeared long before he had arrived at Poisoned Springs.

Like so many men Thorson was a creature with a dark history. He had once ridden with the notorious Wild Bunch and his name and image adorned many a Wanted poster, but that had not concerned his employers. It was difficult to find any sane men willing to work in the remote way stations. The Overland Stagecoach company did not ask many questions when they were hiring. You took what you could get and looked the other way.

It had not taken Thorson long to learn that there was a small fortune to be made in Poisoned Springs if a man was willing to trade anything the Indians wanted for the valuable furs they could provide.

Thorson would supply them with whatever they wanted as long as they continued to bring him their fur pelts, which he then sold to dealers back East. As well as whiskey, which was usually wood spirit with a dash of strong-brewed tea for colour, Thorson also traded guns and ammunition to the increasingly desperate Indians.

His remote way station had another lucrative avenue of profit. It was a safe haven for his fellow wanted outlaws: a place where some of the most deadly wanted men could hide out from the law.

It had not taken long for the land's most notorious gangs to discover that Poisoned Springs was a virtual sanctuary where they were safe. Few sane men ever ventured so close to Indian Territory unless they had no alternative. The lawmen were no exception.

Even though the stagecoaches became less frequent Thorson grew even wealthier. Nothing, it seemed, could spoil the life he had created for himself.

Olin Thorson was soon to be proved wrong.

There was an ancient myth in which many of the tribes that were scattered across the West still believed. It was a story about a silent horseman who rode the land upon a black horse with a silver mane and tail. He was reputed to arrive during lightning storms, when rods of fury were cast down to the earth by angry spirits.

This man was of no known creed. He was not white nor red nor any other colour. He had black hair and eyes the colour of the sky. Some said he was just a myth whilst others claimed that there was a real man who fitted the description of the elusive rider perfectly.

He righted wrongs and never spoke a single word.

Ancient myths can often be confused with reality. The name of the strange avenger varied among the numerous tongues spoken by the many tribes across the West, but when translated into English it always meant the same thing.

Skyhorse.

★   ★   ★

It was the middle of the night and the bar inside the station was full of outlaws all drinking their fill of the whiskey Thorson was only too eager to supply. Every single one of the ten men who propped up the bar was wanted dead or alive.

Rain poured down from the heavens and danced in the porch lantern-light as each of the deadly souls within the wooden building grew increasingly drunk and the storm outside grew ever angrier.

Thunder exploded above the way station as the storm moved slowly towards the forest. The black sky flashed as lightning slithered through the vast expanse of dark, rolling clouds.

It sounded as though there was a war being waged in the violent sky. Perhaps there was. Maybe the gods were angry.

The scurrilous Barton gang had arrived that afternoon after robbing a bank in Waco the previous day. A hundred-mile-long ride was nothing to outlaws who knew that they would be safe once they reached Poisoned Springs.

Each of their saddle-bags was swollen with hundreds of gold coins. The leather satchels, stained with the dried gore of their countless victims, rested against spittoons beside their spurred boots.

Empty whiskey bottles lay on their sides atop the wet bar counter as the outlaws continued to fuel their unquenchable thirsts.

Zack Barton was said to have the largest gang in more than five territories. Each of them was as evil as the next and as black-hearted as the Devil himself.

These were not just outlaws who were wanted dead or alive, they were the scum of the earth. Every one of them had done things no normal man would even contemplate. They had no sense of guilt and had begun to believe that they were immortal. For years they had perpetrated the most hideous of crimes and no lawman's bullet had ever come close to even wounding any of them.

The Devil, it is said, protects his own.

The rain continued to beat down on the tin roof of the porch overhang outside the wide-open doorway of the way station's bar. It sounded as though an army of foot soldiers was marching over the very roof of the building, but none of the whiskey-fuelled outlaws even noticed. They were all far drunker than they imagined.

Yet either sober or drunk made little difference to the Barton gang. The heavily armed men were always like sticks of dynamite that had their fuses lit. At any moment any one of their number could explode into unimaginable fury.

Wisely, Olin Thorson kept the rotgut liquor flowing. He knew from experience that it was the only way to control such creatures.

'How many did you boys kill this time?' Thorson asked.

'Dozens,' Zack Barton replied.

'Did you kill any lawmen?'

The line of men propped against the bar roared in a chorus of laughter. There was no need for any of them to answer the question.

'Keep the whiskey coming, Olin,'

Barton roared as his clenched fist banged down on the counter. 'Our bottles are empty again.'

'It's a good job I had a fresh supply of whiskey brought in last week, Zack.' Thorson reached under the bar counter, heaved up a crate and placed it on its wet surface. He pulled out the black glass bottles and started to slide them along the counter to each of the out-laws. A riotous cheer filled the long room.

'I'll say one thing about you, Olin.' Barton pulled the cork from the fresh bottle before him. 'You always got the best whiskey.'

'I must have known you and the boys were coming, Zack,' Thorson grunted. Then from the corner of his eye he saw something in the porch lantern-light. Something that drew his attention.

He turned his head and recognized two familiar Cheyenne braves riding through the rain towards the hitching pole. Each was astride a small pinto pony. Both had two piles of furs before

10

them. Thorson rubbed his mouth along his sleeve, walked around the counter and marched towards the two Cheyenne braves, who dropped to the ground and carried the piles of furs towards the porch.

'We trade,' one of the warriors said as they both gave the station manager the soaked furs.

'Whiskey?' Thorson asked.

Both of the Cheyennes nodded.

Suddenly Thorson heard Barton's voice boom out behind his broad back.

'Is that stinking Injuns, Olin?'

'Ain't no call for you to get all fired up, Zack,' Thorson said as he turned. 'They're just here to trade.'

Suddenly the darkness lit up as a fork of lightning splintered down from the heavens. The two Cheyennes stopped and looked skywards.

'Get whiskey,' one of them said.

Thorson gave a nod. 'OK, Yellow Feather. You wait here and I'll get you whiskey.'

Zack Barton disliked every colour of

man except white. He pushed Thorson aside and walked to the edge of the porch boards. His fiery eyes burned down at the two bedraggled braves.

Barton gritted his teeth and glared at both the Indians in turn. 'You ain't getting no whiskey. Me and my boys are gonna drink the whole lot of it. Savvy?'

'Leave them be. They're just trading furs for whiskey, Zack.' Thorson walked back to the counter and dropped the furs close to the black-bellied stove. He was about to pick up two bottles of his home-made whiskey when he saw Barton draw one of his guns and fan its hammer. Two deafening shots echoed around the interior of the station building.

Barton was grinning widely as he returned to the counter.

'What you do that for?' Thorson gasped in stunned horror.

The leader of the outlaws stared at Thorson. The smile evaporated. 'They was just Injuns, Olin. Filthy stinking Injuns.'

'You damn fool,' Thorson raged at

Barton. 'You'll bring the whole damn tribe down on us.'

Barton glared at Thorson. 'Let them come. I ain't feared of no redskins. Let them come.'

Thorson felt his throat tighten as if a noose had been pulled around his neck. He said nothing.

One by one the other outlaws walked to the porch and also fired down at the dead Indians. Each one returned with the same satisfied look on his face.

'You don't know what you've just done,' Thorson said.

'We intend drinking all of your damn whiskey ourselves, Olin,' Barton told him, filling his glass with the amber-coloured liquor before downing it. 'Any objections?'

'Nope.' Thorson shrugged as he stared at the ten hardened outlaws who faced him. 'Reckon we all gotta die sometime. I just figured I'd die with my hair still on my head.'

Then as another mighty thunderclap shook the wooden building each of the men noticed another horse being steered towards the hitching rail. It was guided between the pair of ponies, then hauled to a halt.

'Who the hell is that?' one of the outlaws asked, vainly trying to focus through the smoke.

Olin Thorson screwed up his eyes and looked at the horse and rider. He felt his heart quicken. There was something about the look of the horseman that he seemed to recall.

Barton stared at Thorson. 'You look like you just seen a ghost, Olin.'

'Maybe I just have,' Thorson gasped as he recalled the stories he had heard many times since he had traded with the Indians from the forest.

'What you mean?'

'Look, Zack. That critter's horse looks like the one in stories I've heard the Indians talking about,' Thorson said nervously. 'A black horse with a silver mane and tail ain't right. There ain't such a horse, is there?'

'Are you going loco?' Barton eased

himself around and looked at the horseman standing like a statue between the two dead Cheyennes. The man stepped up on to the porch. 'The horse is just wet. It probably ain't black at all.'

'Who is he?' one of the outlaws asked, lowering the bottle from his lips. 'Is he a lawman?'

'Whoever that critter is he sure ain't gonna live too much longer, boys,' Barton said, and chuckled.

Thorson began to shake. He edged his way along the bar counter until he reached the shotgun he kept propped up against a barrel of beer. He grabbed the hefty weapon and checked its twin chambers before cocking its barrels.

'Who is he?' Barton snarled at Thorson again. 'Answer me, you fat bastard. Who is that?'

'Skyhorse,' Thorson gulped.

One of the other outlaws pushed away from the bar. 'There ain't no such critter, Olin.'

The tall stranger was soaked to his skin. He stood in the frame of the door.

His hands hovered over his two holstered guns as his small blue eyes darted their gaze from one wanted outlaw to the other.

Barton and his men moved away from the counter and glared at the strange man who stood defiantly before them.

'They say your name's Skyhorse,' Barton snarled at the man. 'Is that right? Are you Skyhorse?'

The man gave a slight nod of his head.

'Looks something like an Injun to me, Zack,' another of the outlaws said.

'He sure ain't dressed like no Injun,' a third member of the gang said. 'Looks a tad like a Chinaman, or maybe a Mexican.'

'Nah, he's an Injun.'

'Yeah, he sure does look like a damn Injun.' Barton drew both his guns. 'Kill him.'

All of the outlaws slapped leather. The lantern-light danced across the barrels of the weapons as they were drawn from their holsters.

Before any of the weapons could be

16

fired the stranger had drawn, cocked and started firing his own two six-shooters. One by one the outlaws fell to the ground. Within a few heartbeats every one of the gang lay dead in the sawdust.

Only Olin Thorson remained alive as the tall stranger stared with narrowed eyes through the gunsmoke at the man behind the bar.

Thorson swung around and pulled both triggers of the shotgun, but the stranger had dropped down on to one knee. As half of the wall behind him was turned into smouldering splinters the stranger fired.

Thorson felt the lethal bullet hit him in the centre of his chest. He knew he was already dead as he staggered towards the stranger, who had risen back to his full height. The burly man crashed on to his knees as blood pumped from the neat hole in his shirt front.

'Are you Skyhorse?' Thorson croaked as gore trailed from the corner of his mouth. 'Are you?'

Skyhorse nodded.

'I knew it was you.' Thorson fell forwards.

The tall stranger reloaded his guns swiftly, then holstered them. He looked down at one of the saddle-bags and the gleaming coins within its open satchel. He leaned over, plucked eleven golden coins from it and pushed them into his damp trail-coat pocket.

As he walked back to the door he paused for a moment and looked back down at Olin Thorson's dead body.

'My name's Joe Skyhorse,' he muttered in a low, rasping whisper. 'Funny how you knew me considering we never met before.'

Lightning flashed outside as Skyhorse strode back out into the rain towards his black mount. He holstered both his guns, took hold of the silver mane of the horse and mounted the handsome animal.

He turned the stallion to face the trail that led into the perilous Indian Territory. He then rode fearlessly towards the forest.

1

Black smoke billowed up into the blue heavens from the twin stacks of the riverboat as it stood in the mouth of the deep estuary next to the quayside. Mooring ropes were hauled and secured by muscular arms until the huge vessel was brought close to the dry land. Its paddle wheel came to a reluctant halt and its gangplanks were lowered on to the southernmost section of the prosperous settlement of Black River. Hundreds of labourers went about their back-breaking rituals as the boat's passengers gathered in preparation for disembarkation.

The vessel had travelled up from the Mexican Gulf to the town where wealthy businessmen gathered to bid for the vast herds of cattle that were bought and sold every few months.

It was not just the well-heeled who

visited Black River. Any town where money was in abundance drew all sorts of people from every corner of the country. The large number of saloons and gambling-halls were proof of that simple fact. Yet not all those who stared down from the riverboat had travelled to Black River for honest reasons.

Three tall men who appeared to be cut from the same cloth watched with hard, cruel eyes as their fellow passengers scurried on to the shore. At first their well-tailored outer dress seemed no different from that of other men who had arrived in their Sunday best. On closer inspection concealed weaponry could be seen under the tails of their long coats.

These were not businessmen like so many who had travelled to Black River. These were men who had a different line of work, which paid just as well as most and often a lot better.

The three Horton brothers were specialists.

Earl, Luke and Will Horton were

hired killers: the highest-paid assassins in the territory. They had made their way from the serene Eastern shores, where they had discovered at an early age that their ability and eagerness to kill for money could earn them a small fortune. The Hortons had soon realized that there were only so many men you could kill before you became the hunted and no longer the hunter. For vengeance was a price all hired killers had eventually to cope with. Every man they had killed had kinfolk who wanted revenge. It did not take long before the Horton brothers realized they had to venture further afield in order to continue plying their lethal trade.

Unlike many they had not ventured West but journeyed down the country from port to port. Each seaport offered them fresh prey and new paymasters.

It had taken two profitable years for them to reach Black River and it was no accident that they were in the cattle-trading town.

Earl Horton was barely four years

older than his youngest brother Will, yet he seemed twice the age of his two siblings. He made all the decisions for the trio of hired killers.

The Hortons never went anywhere without their prized horses. Even when travelling by ship or riverboat the brothers paid passage for their thoroughbreds, for they were the key to their operations. A man could not rely upon a hired saddle horse when his very life depended upon the speed of a reliable mount.

'Get the horses, Luke,' Earl whispered to his brother.

Luke Horton did as he was told, walking to the nearest companionway and heading down the steps.

Earl pulled out a silver cigar case and flicked its hinged lid open. He withdrew a thin cigar and placed it between his teeth, then returned the valuable case to his frock-coat pocket.

'I'll get the bags from our cabin, Earl,' Will said.

Earl struck a match and touched the

end of the cigar. He sucked in smoke, then gave a slow nod as it filled his lungs.

He said nothing as his youngest sibling walked away in the direction of the cabin they had shared. Earl Horton just stared out at the quayside, watching the activity with the keen interest of an eagle deciding upon its next prey.

There were many buggies of varying value but one stood out in its splendour. A black carriage with golden decoration waited slightly apart from the activity. A pair of matched greys held in check by a driver in full livery made the hired killer nod to himself.

Earl Horton knew that had to be the man by whom he and his brothers had been hired.

Smoke drifted from his teeth and a deadly smile etched his hardened features.

'Reckon it's about time you and me set eyes on one another, Mr Solomon Casey,' Horton muttered to himself, and strode to the top of the companion-way. His long legs started down the steps to where dozens of sweating men laboured as they carried hefty bales off the bow of the boat amid disembarking passengers of every shape and size. Earl Horton aimed his polished boots at the gangplank.

With every stride of his long legs the leader of the trio of hired assassins continued to stare at the carriage. He did not blink as cigar smoke drifted from his mouth. The gaze of his narrowed eyes burned across the distance between himself and the door of the black vehicle.

A white-gloved hand rested upon the highly laquered rim of the door. A large diamond ring sparkled as he closed the distance between them.

Horton stopped a few yards from the carriage.

'Solomon Casey?' he called out.

The gloved hand pushed the carriage door open. 'Get in.'

2

Solomon Casey looked across his wide
desk at the three gunmen he had
summoned and liked what he saw. Each
of the brothers had the same square jaw
and dark hair and it was impossible to
tell which of them was actually the
tallest. The Horton brothers were all far
taller than anyone the shrewd banker
had ever encountered before. Their
elegant attire gave no inkling as to what
their profession actually was.

Yet the rotund man, who not only
ran the town's largest bank but owned
it as well, knew that he had chosen his
hired assassins shrewdly. Only men who
were experts at their profession ever
dressed with such refinement. Each of
the brothers inspired confidence in the
elderly banker as he gestured towards a
decanter of brandy set beside expensive
crystal tumblers.

'Would you care for a drink, gentlemen?' Casey asked. He clipped the tip off a fat cigar and inhaled its aroma beneath his nose.

Earl Horton was seated between his siblings; he eased himself forwards until his eyes locked on to those of their paymaster. He gave a slight shake of his head.

'We never drink before a job, Mr Casey,' he explained.

The banker struck a match and raised it to his cigar. He puffed like a locomotive until the office was enveloped in a cloud of smoke.

'I like that,' Casey said, dropping the spent match into a glass ashtray between them. 'That shows dedication and more than a hint of professionalism. It's obvious that you boys take your work seriously.'

Earl smiled. 'We have to. When folks in our trade don't take their work seriously, they usually end up dead.'

'Indeed.' Casey sucked on the cigar as if it were a nipple for a few seconds, then he too leaned forwards. His eyes were hidden by bags both above and below the brown orbs, but they were as intense as those of the three hired gunmen before him. 'I imagine you'd like to know whom I have brought you here to dispose of, gentlemen?'

The three brothers all nodded at exactly the same moment.

'To kill,' Earl Horton corrected.

'Indeed.' Casey shrugged.

The brothers sat and watched the banker. Luke Horton kept tapping his fingers nervously on the arm of his chair as if eager to get on with the job which had brought them to Black River.

'Have any of you heard of a cattle ranch called the Lazy B?' Casey asked through a cloud of smoke.

They all shook their heads.

'Nope. We're new to this part of the country,' Earl said.

Casey carefully tapped his ash into the glass tray. 'Then neither have you heard of the man who owns it. His name is Judge Nathan Berkley.'

Will looked at his eldest brother. 'I don't reckon we ought to tangle with no judge, Earl. We might find ourselves in a barrel of hot water if we kill one of them critters.'

Earl Horton's face was expressionless. 'Let Mr Casey finish, Will.'

The youngest of the Horton boys relaxed. He returned his eyes to the banker. 'Sorry, Mr Casey. Carry on.'

Casey gave a nod and pushed the cigar in to the corner of his mouth. His fingers interlocked as though in mocking prayer.

'Berkley has been a thorn in my side for twenty years,' he started, 'but he is not the man I wish to have killed.'

'Then who do you want us to kill?' Earl Horton wondered.

'Have you ever heard of a man called James Henry King?' The banker watched their faces but saw no recognition in any of them as they pondered the name.

'It ain't a handle I've come across,' Earl said.

'Me neither.' Luke shrugged.

The youngest brother just shook his head silently.

'Who is he?' Earl asked.

Solomon Casey smiled. 'He's the one man who has kept the judge planted on the Lazy B and prevented the old man from selling up. Berkley has always treated King like a son. The old man intends leaving the entire ranch to King when he eventually dies and that is something I do not intend to allow.'

'Why not?' Will Horton looked puzzled.

The eldest of the brothers was far sharper than his siblings and grasped what the banker was implying. He raised a finger and wagged it at Casey. 'I think I know what you're getting at, Mr Casey. If the judge dies then King inherits the ranch. King must be young and he'll never sell the Lazy B in your lifetime. Right?'

'Exactly.' The banker sighed.

'But if King dies first then you think that Berkley will sell up,' Earl added.

Luke Horton frowned. 'What was King's name again?'

'James Henry King,' Casey repeated.

Luke patted his elder brother's arm. 'Appaloosa King.'

'That's what people call him.' The banker nodded and again tapped ash into the tray before him. 'So you have heard of him?'

The expression on Earl Horton's face suddenly went grim as he chewed on the name his brother had just uttered. He rubbed his jaw and looked at the banker.

'We've all heard of Appaloosa King,' Earl said drily.

Solomon Casey adjusted himself in his chair. 'Does that make a difference?'

'Yep, it sure does,' Earl Horton said. 'It means the price just doubled.'

Solomon Casey rose to his feet and stared at the notorious Horton brothers. His right hand shook as he pointed his cigar at the hired gunmen.

'You want double?' he raged. 'But King is just a cowpuncher. A stinking cowpuncher. Why would you want double to kill him? Why?'

Earl Horton rose to his feet, grabbed the banker's collar and hauled him towards him. His icy stare drilled into the irate banker.

'Because he's Appaloosa King, Mr Casey,' Horton snarled, and pushed their paymaster back down on to his padded leather chair. 'We've tangled with him before. He might be a lotta things but he ain't just a cowpuncher.'

3

The Lazy B Ranch was big like the men who lived upon its fertile soil. To the west of the huge cattle spread lay an arid, mostly uncharted terrain, whilst to the east a forested territory was still home to several Indian tribes. This was a place few white men ever ventured into and lived to tell the tale. Kiowa and Cheyenne braves tolerated one another but they had no liking for those they blamed for forcing them from their ancestral homelands. Once they had roamed freely like the buffalo and had not been confined.

That was a candle which would never be rekindled.

The large ranch stood alone on the outskirts of the town of Black River. There were no other ranches anywhere near the size of Judge Berkley's. Yet even though the longhorn steers had brought prosperity to the region there were many men like Solomon Casey who wanted to get their hands upon it.

Land meant power and there were many who craved power more than anything else. Their desire and greed became their only reason to exist.

At the heart of the ranch a large house stood proudly, as it had done since its construction decades earlier. Berkley seldom ventured away from the impressive mansion since age had at last taken its toll on his once strong frame. He entrusted everything to the young man he had raised as though he were his son.

James Henry King had learned everything his mentor had taught him with an eagerness few other cowboys could have equalled. He had become the ranch foreman because of his total loyalty to the judge. If Berkley considered Appaloosa his son then the young man also thought of the elderly judge as his father. He, like so many of his age, had never known any real parents.

Berkley was still the brains of the Lazy B.

Appaloosa King was the body.

It was a partnership that had proved profitable.

A score of cowboys were required to control the vast herd of longhorn steers the two men had bred over the years. The ranges were filled with them and twice a year King and his fellow Lazy B cowboys would cut out a quarter of their number and drive them north to the nearest railhead.

Yet even though the two men who controlled the cattle ranch thought they knew everything about one another, each had his secrets.

Secrets neither had ever burdened the other with.

The afternoon sun was hot as it blazed down upon the array of buildings scattered around the court-yard of the ranch. The old judge sat under the porch veranda outside the large door of the house and watched the activity in which he was no longer able to participate. It had become a ritual.

With clouds of dust kicking up from his stallion's hoofs, Appaloosa King came riding from the south atop one of his precious mounts towards the old man. Berkley smiled at the welcome sight. A sight he never tired of.

The sheer skill of the intrepid horseman never failed to amaze the older man. Berkley had once been a pretty fine rider himself but he had never been able to control a horse the way Appaloosa could.

King dragged rein and stopped the fiery appaloosa a few yards from the ranch house. Within a heartbeat the cowboy had dismounted and looped his reins around the hitching rail below the seated judge.

'Howdy, Judge,' the dust-caked rider greeted the older man.

'Where have you been, son?' Berkley asked as he chewed on the stem of his pipe.

Appaloosa unbuckled his chaps and

stepped up on to the porch. He draped the dusty leathers over the low rail and sat down on the whitewashed wood-work.

'I've been checking the stock down in the lower pastures, Judge,' King replied. He removed his hat and ran his sleeve across his brow.

Berkley nodded. 'Do you reckon we ought to use the steers from down there on the next drive, son?'

The cowboy nodded. 'Yep. Trouble is I figure we've lost at least fifty head since I was down there last.'

The judge smiled. 'Them Indians get hungry, son. I've always turned a blind eye to them taking the odd steer. They never take more than they need to feed their families.'

Appaloosa King inhaled deeply. 'They must have taken hundreds of the critters over the years, Judge.'

Berkley nodded. 'More like thou-sands.'

'Some men would take exception to having their steers stolen, Judge.' King removed his spurs and placed them on his chaps.

'Some men are fools.'

The younger man stood up and was about to enter the house when the judge's hand reached from the chair and took hold of Appaloosa's arm. The cowboy paused and looked down at the frail shadow of the man he had known for two thirds of his own life.

'What's wrong, Judge?'

'I need to talk to you,' Berkley said.

'We always talk, Judge.' King smiled.

Judge Berkley turned his eyes away from the man he considered his son. 'I know, but this time I've got something mighty important to tell you. Something really serious.'

King could see the concern in the judge's wrinkled eyes. It was a rare sight, which took the cowboy by surprise.

'I'm listening, Judge.'

'Take me inside,' Berkley instructed. 'I don't want anyone else to hear what I have to tell you.'

King grinned. 'Is it a secret?'

The older man looked up at King's face.

'In a way it has been a secret for most of my sorrowful life, son. It's time I told you something nobody has ever had an inkling of.' Berkley sighed.

'Sounds important, Judge.' Appaloosa King placed his hat back on the crown of his head and reached down. He scooped the old man up in his arms and carried him indoors. It seemed to the cowboy that the once powerful figure was getting lighter with every passing day.

King walked across the large room as Sean Finnigan, the cook, laid out cutlery on the long table. Appaloosa looked at the cook and Finnigan headed back into the kitchen.

As Berkley was carefully placed on a soft armchair next to an unlit fire he looked hard at King.

'We've never spoken about our early days,' the judge said, sliding his pipe into his vest pocket.

King dragged a hardback chair from the dining table and sat astride it. 'Everybody got themselves private times they don't hanker to talk about, Judge. Sometimes it don't pay to burden friends with things long gone.'

'You've always been wiser than your years, Appaloosa,' the judge said. 'I agree with you that some things are best kept to oneself, but times change and sometimes we have to change with them.'

King smiled. 'I wish I knew what's eating at you, Judge.'

Berkley leaned back in his comfortable chair. 'As I said, things change. Things we thought were long forgotten sometimes come back to haunt us.'

The cowboy looked concerned. 'Is somebody from your past trying to hurt you, Judge? Is that it? Tell me who they are and I'll go and teach them a lesson.'

Berkley gave a chuckle. 'You've always been the protector, son. I'm obliged but that ain't it at all. Nobody is trying to hurt me. This ain't bad news.'

'It ain't?' Appaloosa removed his hat and threw it aside.

Nathan Berkley shook his head. 'No, son. What I've got to tell you is something I've tried to forget for the last twenty-five years.'

The cowboy leaned back. He could not hide the troubled expression that etched his dust-caked features.

'I'm starting to get troubled, Judge. What kind of secret would someone like you be sitting on for twenty-five years? Spit it out.'

Judge Berkley looked at King. 'I was married for a few years before I headed West, son.'

'Married?' Appaloosa gasped in total shock. Of all the things he expected his mentor to say, that was not one of them.

Berkley nodded. 'Yep, I was married to a real fine young lady from back East, but she didn't like being away from her rich folks in this country. It was mighty wild back then and she headed back to the safety and comforts she was used to. I was scratching a living and she wasn't made for that. She up and left me.'

Appaloosa scratched his chin thoughtfully. 'You never mentioned anything about having a wife. I'd have remembered that for sure.'

'There are some failures a man don't like telling anyone about, son.' Berkley smiled.

'Hell, it weren't your fault she couldn't cut it out here, Judge,' King said. 'Not many females can. They have to have a certain kinda grit. Reckon fine ladies have all the grit bred out of them.'

'That might be it.'

Appaloosa tilted his head. He could tell that Berkley had not finished his unexpected confession. 'There's something else, ain't there? Something you ain't spat out yet. What is it, Judge?'

'A few days back I received a letter from Boston,' Berkley revealed.

'From your wife?'

'Nope.' The judge continued to smile thoughtfully. 'From my daughter.'

'You've got a daughter?' King swallowed hard.

Judge Berkley clasped his hands. 'It would seem so.'

★ ★ ★

It was cool and tranquil inside the forest as the lone rider Joe Skyhorse rode along a narrow riverbed. There had been no sign of any of the numerous Indians who filled its vast expanse since the man astride the black mount with the silver mane and tail had entered. Yet Skyhorse knew they were there, watching his steady progress with curious eyes.

The first hint that he was not alone had been when the forest had fallen silent shortly after sunrise. That was not normal and he knew it. The horseman had ridden through many similar landscapes before and there was always noise. Skyhorse realized that the only time the birds and animals fell silent was when there were hunters in the vicinity.

Although Skyhorse rode with his head bowed he was fully aware of everything that surrounded him. His eyes darted from side to side as each small sound attracted his keen attention.

The brim of his pale hat covered most of his face, but he still saw and heard everything. As the tall, elegant stallion stepped from the shallow river up on to the riverbank Skyhorse was fully aware that he was surrounded, yet there was no evidence of concern in his long, lean frame.

Like the fearless warriors he knew were watching his every move, he was unafraid. He tapped his spurs against the flanks of the impressive animal to urge it on through the shafts of golden sunlight that filtered down through the thick, leafy canopy far above him. With each step of his mount the horseman tried to recall what and who he really was.

It had been months since he had found himself at the foot of a mountain, yet a small scar above his left eyebrow was the only evidence of his accident. The horse had been standing guard over him as he had regained consciousness and Skyhorse had assumed it belonged to him.

In truth he had no memory of anything before that moment and even the name he used was one he had found written on a scrap of paper buried deep in the stallion's saddlebags.

Was it his true name? Did the horse even belong to him?

There was no way of knowing. All Joe Skyhorse could do was continue riding in a vain attempt to one day remember an entire lifetime that had disappeared. The further he rode the more he doubted that there had been a life prior to his awakening beside the strange horse.

He was a man without a past, yet everyone he encountered seemed to know him. When they looked into his face it was as though they saw their own reflection.

His appearance seemed to mimic all known races of men spread across the vast continent. He looked similar and yet unlike all others in equal proportions.

Skyhorse was someone whom it was impossible to pigeonhole.

Yet there was something else about the strange, quiet rider who travelled through Indian Territory. There was a curious aura that set him apart and troubled all those who looked upon his handsome features.

Since the day he had first awoken beside the protective stallion he had heard the vague stories of the heavenly horseman after whom he was named. The further he travelled the more confused he became.

Could the stories be true?

Was he just the figment of other

people's imagination? He tried to remember, but there was no memory left inside his young mind. It was as though he been born the moment he had awoken beside the handsome stallion.

That was the only thing that troubled Joe Skyhorse.

There was an empty void of a life that may never have even existed at all. He tapped his spurs and continued to guide his horse through the dense forest.

The trees were close together as the black horse reached a slight rise. Their canopies almost blocked out the sun high above the horseman as he drew rein and stopped his mount.

His keen hearing told him that there were at least thirty braves encircling him, but Skyhorse showed no concern as he looped his reins around his saddle horn and removed his hat.

He shook his black hair free and knew that every eye was focused upon his unusual features. Again the arrows and bullets did not seek or find him. He hung the hat by its drawstring from the grip of one of his holstered guns and slowly dismounted.

Once more he was the object of curiosity.

He removed his jacket and placed it over his saddle as his eyes watched and his ears listened. He could hear them moving around in the dense undergrowth.

It was not the first time he had encountered curious eyes and he knew it would not be the last. For some reason he always drew a crowd.

He wanted to see them and let them see him. He posed no danger to those who meant him no harm. It was only those who tried to kill him who tasted his wrath. Like the outlaws who had killed the two Indians outside the way station and then tried to do the same to him.

There was only one thing he could do to draw them out into the open. He would simply sit down and wait for them to move from the cover of the trees and brush.

Defiantly Joe Skyhorse dropped down at the nose of his horse and leaned his back against a tree trunk. He folded his arms and closed his eyes.

Within a few moments he could hear the moccasin-covered feet approaching from all sides. He remained motionless and listened.

They came closer and closer. He could almost hear their hearts pounding like war drums inside their buckskin-covered chests, yet he did not move a muscle.

Then, when he was sure that they were all within twenty feet of him, Skyhorse opened his eyes. They seemed startled and abruptly stopped at the sight of his vivid blue eyes. There were far more of them than he had imagined. At least fifty Cheyenne braves of various ages surrounded him.

Skyhorse remained perfectly still. His eyes wandered from one of them to another. Every single one of them, even the youngest, carried a bow.

Every arrow was trained upon him.

One of the older braves, whom Skyhorse took to be either a medicine man or a chief, began to rant at him. He sounded angrier than all of the others put together. The seated youngster looked up at him and raised an eyebrow.

Then the ranting stopped.

The angry brave was looking at the stallion. He pointed at the animal and seemed to explain something to the other warriors. Skyhorse knew it concerned his black horse with the silver mane and tail.

When the medicine man stopped talking he pointed a tomahawk down at Skyhorse and muttered a single word.

Within seconds every one of the other Cheyennes repeated the same word.

The young rider got back to his feet and glanced at their faces. He had seen the same look in many other men's faces before. It was a mixture of fear and total awe.

'What's the matter?' Skyhorse asked.

The medicine man raised a hand. 'You are Skyhorse.'

'Yep, reckon I am.'

4

There were many hotels in the sprawling settlement of Black River. Hotels of every imaginable kind, from weathered wooden structures to fine stone edifices. Each catered for its customers according to the size of their wallets. The cheapest were close to the water's edge, whilst the most expensive were situated in the town square. Yet they all served the same purpose, no matter what the cost of the bed provided might be.

The grandest of all the hotels was called by an equally grand name. The Palace stood directly opposite the town hall and a church. All the hotels had been built with imported stone and carved to rival anything found on the eastern seaboard. The Palace had only been open for business a mere eighteen months but it proved itself a favourite with those with more money than sense. An average man would have had to work for a month in order to pay for one night's room and board in the ornate and luxurious Palace.

Only the richest of guests stayed in the Palace. Nobody else could ever afford their breathtaking prices. Yet to the trio of hired assassins the price of their suite of rooms meant nothing. They were rich, even though their fortune might only be temporary, for they had already managed to negotiate the doubling of their blood money.

The two younger Horton boys moved around the suite of rooms in wonder at the splendour their deadly profession earned them, whilst the eldest brother made his way to the most central of the bedrooms.

Earl Horton sat down on the edge of his plush bed and unfolded a detailed map he had obtained down in the hotel lobby. As his brothers investigated the suite of rooms the deadliest of the gunmen simply studied the map.

Until Solomon Casey had revealed who their target was, Earl Horton had not had any doubts that he and his brothers would simply execute their victim and move on. Having learned that Appaloosa King was the man Casey wanted killed, the eldest of the brothers was now troubled.

Three years earlier they had encountered the cowboy with the strange name. They had underestimated him then and it had nearly cost them their own lives. Earl chewed on his cigar as smoke tormented his narrowed eyes. He recalled the rider on the strange horse with the spotted rump. It had been the only time that he and his brothers had failed to fulfil their deadly agreement.

They had failed because of Appaloosa King.

Earl Horton did not want to make the same mistake again. This time he had to ensure that the cowboy did not outwit them. This time King had to die, but the lethal assassin knew that men like him did not die easy.

There had to be a foolproof plan. You could never afford to make a single mistake with men like Appaloosa King.

His eyes studied the large map with an intensity only birds of prey could equal. He absorbed every little detail and memorized it. The map was the key, his determined brain kept telling him.

They were venturing into an unfamiliar territory, which their chosen prey knew like the back of his hand. Earl Horton had to know it as well as King obviously did if he were to be able to get the better of the cowboy.

There was no room for error.

At last, after what seemed like an eternity to Earl, his brothers joined him in the beautifully decorated room and seated themselves.

'What ya looking at, Earl?' Will asked.

Earl glanced across at the youngest of his kin. 'This is a map of the entire area, Will.'

'What we need a map for?' Luke enquired.

'How else are we going to figure where Appaloosa is?' Earl growled.

'We know he's on some ranch called the Lazy B, Earl,' Will said. 'That fat old banker told us that.'

'So we just ride there and kill him,' Luke added.

'There could be twenty or more cowpunchers on that ranch, you dumb bastard,' Earl snapped. 'That's a lot of bullets headed in our direction. Nope, we have to get him on his lonesome.'

'We ain't used a map before,' Will observed.

'We are this time.' Earl dropped the unfolded map on the carpet and spread it out. 'Look at the area north of Black River, boys. The ranch is vast and this map ain't got much detail. Look at the land around the ranch. That's Injun territory and we ain't tangling with no redskins. Appaloosa might be on the ranch, but where?'

'We have to lure him out,' Luke said.

'How?' Earl exhaled. 'We have to study this damn map and get used to the land. We have to know every canyon and every trail if we're going to get this killing done right, boys. This is a mighty dangerous job we've undertaken. If we get it wrong it'll be us who ends up dead and not Appaloosa.'

'I got me an idea,' Will suggested. 'What if we send a telegram to Appaloosa and get him to come here?'

The eldest of the brothers nodded. 'That's half of a good idea, Will. We send him a wire, not to come here but to go somewhere else. Somewhere on this damn map. Somewhere remote where we can bushwhack him.'

'Where?' Luke frowned as he bent over and stared at the colourful map.

'Yeah, where?' Will sighed.

Suddenly Earl Horton grinned and stabbed a finger at the paper. 'There.'

5

The judge looked across the wide room at the only one of his ranch hands who was not consuming the mouth-watering supper that his cook had prepared. As was his habit when troubled or simply confused, Appaloosa King stood before the large window and stared out at the impressive view before him. He had always tried to find answers in the scenery and sometimes he had found them.

He heard the old rancher labour as he made his way across the room with the aid of two sturdy walking sticks. King turned and reached out to help the elderly rancher.

'Don't fret, son,' Berkley said in a voice he knew would calm down the anxious cowboy. 'I can make it to the window.'

The young cowboy bit his lip and

watched as the older man reached a hardback chair and eased his crippled body down upon it. Berkley gave out a long sigh and looked up at the cowboy's face.

'Cookie will be mighty sore when he sees that you haven't touched the steak he cooked for you, Appaloosa,' Berkley said. He leaned back and blinked several times. 'The rest of the boys seem to be enjoying their supper. How come you ain't eating?'

Appaloosa raised an eyebrow. 'I could ask you the same question, Judge. You ain't touched your supper either.'

Judge Berkley shrugged. 'Yeah, I know. Sometimes a man has to think rather than eat. Right?'

Appaloosa nodded and rested a hip on the wooden sill of the window. 'Guess you kinda took the wind out of my sails when you said you have a daughter. Reckon I must be surprised. In all the years I've known you, you've never once mentioned the fact that you had been married once or had a daughter, Judge. How come?'

Berkley looked at the eyes of his young friend. 'I was married young. Too young. She was a spoiled only child and didn't like it here. She left me and I never heard from her again.'

King leaned closer to the wrinkled face of Berkley. 'You didn't know that you were a father, did you?'

'Nope.' The judge sighed. 'I never even had a clue that I'd fathered anyone. My wife never contacted me again. I tried to wipe the memory of that marriage out of my mind. I succeeded for a real long time until I got that letter from my daughter.'

'What's her name?'

'Catherine.'

'Why'd she write to you now, Judge?'

'Her mother died,' Berkley answered. 'She was looking through her mother's papers and discovered the truth. She wrote to tell me that she was heading here even though she knows that she might be just visiting another tombstone.'

'When is she due?' Appaloosa asked.

'By my figuring she ought to be arriving at Deadlock in the next week or so, son,' the judge whispered, and glanced over his shoulder at the rest of the ranch hands at the table.

King gave a knowing nod. 'Deadlock is the closest railhead to the Lazy B. It's still a hell of a long way from here, though. That's a rough trail between here and there for anyone to travel.'

Berkley looked concerned. 'I'm not happy about her having to travel all the way from Deadlock to here on her lonesome, Appaloosa.'

The young cowboy bit his lower lip. 'It is a real dangerous trail. A female alone would make a mighty tempting target for a whole lot of folks.'

'That's why I was thinking that maybe you and a few of the boys ought to ride to Deadlock to meet and escort her here, son.' The judge stared through his spectacles at the cowboy.

'I don't want to take too many boys with me, Judge,' King said, rising back to his full height. 'Maybe just two, so we don't draw attention to ourselves.'

Judge Berkley smiled. 'When do you intend going?'

'Not until I've eaten that juicy steak and downed me a few cups of black coffee, Judge,' the cowboy replied. Then he leaned over and helped the older man back to his feet. 'Reckon we'll make better progress if we ride by night.'

'Who do you intend taking with you?'

King's eyes darted at the dozen or so cowboys seated around the long dining table. They focused on two of the youngest. Billy Smith and Dobie Giles were only a few years beyond their twentieth birthdays and both were skilled horsemen.

'Billy and Dobie,' King said loud enough to draw the attention of both the ranch hands.

The young cowboys looked up at King as he helped the judge down on to his chair at the table.

'What you chewing on our names for,

Appaloosa?' Billy asked the grinning ranch foreman.

'I was just telling the judge that I'm taking you two sidewinders to Deadlock with me,' Appaloosa answered. He sat down and dragged his plate towards him.

'What we going to Deadlock for?' Dobie queried.

'We have to pick up a package for the judge.' King smiled as he sliced through his steak. His eyes darted from one of the young cowboys to the other. 'A mighty important one.'

6

An ever-changing panorama of unexpected awesomeness was something the handsome female had never before witnessed. It was beyond description in its breathtaking magnificence and something that she found impossible to look away from for more than a few heartbeats. Not even the greatest of poets could have managed to capture the ever-changing vision in words. This was something that had to be seen. All of the romantic words she had learned in her life had not prepared her for this.

Her mind raced as it vainly tried to absorb what her eyes were looking at through the large carriage window. She tried to accept that this was real. The incredible scenery was no glimpse into a wondrous dream: it was real.

The mighty locomotive spewed black plumes of twisting smoke up into the vast sky, which dominated the plains as the train continued its steady and relentless journey along the gleaming rail tracks towards the still-distant Deadlock. The sun was low and on the opposite side of the train from where she was seated. The dark shadow of the train and its trailing cars moved on the uneven ground below her uninterrupted view. It was hypnotic and quite relaxing. For days she had travelled and stared out at the scenery in wonder. Soon the journey would be at an end, but she did not want it ever to stop.

Her eyes squinted as she attempted to see everything there was to be seen. It was a strange and unfamiliar sight for the beautiful eyes of the petite, elegantly attired female who sat in a blue velvet dress beside the window of the passenger car.

Catherine Berkley had grown used to the sights of red-brick and concrete buildings which were neatly set in blocks of equal sizes. She was used to seeing people of every description filling avenues of streets. There were no people of any sort to be seen here. She had glimpsed animals far off in the distance, but no people.

It was unnerving and yet soothing to someone who had grown used to crowds. The sight that she had beheld since leaving the comfort of her Eastern home now totally amazed her. Mile after mile and hour after hour it seemed that between the railroad towns there was just nothing but handsome vistas.

Since she had set out on a journey of discovery she had seen every imaginable natural sight. Mountains higher than even the tallest building had been the first thing to astonish her. Then forests so large that some seemed to go on for days as the train forged on. Then she had seen a different landscape in contrast with everything that she had witnessed previously. It was one of rolling plains and ranges, which stretched from horizon to horizon.

In just a few days Catherine had

travelled through all four seasons and still things were changing. The temperature was increasing and making her wonder whether she was suitably dressed for her ultimate destination. It had been cold when she had set out from her now distant home. Now it was getting warmer and warmer with each passing moment.

Catherine was thankful for having made the decision to pay for the private room inside the lavishly appointed carriage, but wondered if she had been wise to travel alone. What if all the stories about the Wild West were true? How did women survive in these lands?

A chilling thought made her well-hidden bosom heave.

Was there any law to protect females in places like Deadlock? She tried to dismiss the question, but it remained there in the back of her mind.

Had she made the biggest mistake of her life? Should she have waited for her father to reply? What if he was dead, like her mother?

Again she tried to force the fears out of her mind. Once more she failed.

This was no short journey across town from home to the theatre, such as she was used to. This was no simple shopping expedition where there were police officers on virtually every corner.

This was an epic trek that she had undertaken.

Even in her wildest imaginings Catherine had never dreamt how long it would take to reach the man she had only learned about after the death of her mother.

The discovery that her father was not dead had come as a shock to someone who had never once doubted the word of her prim and proper mother. To realize that there was a man somewhere out in the virtually untamed West who had no idea that he even had a daughter astounded Catherine.

For years the beautiful young woman had believed that her mother was a widow. Few words had ever been spoken about the man who had fathered her. None of her wealthy family had ever mentioned anything about the mysterious Judge Nathan Berkley, apart from the fact that he had taken his sophisticated wife to a hostile, brutal land where savages slaughtered the innocent.

As the black smoke floated past the carriage window the young woman wondered how many other lies had been told to her over her lifetime.

No one should ever learn that their entire life was built on an untruth, she thought. Why had her mother abandoned her father? Why had she told her that he was dead? It made no sense to Catherine.

She sighed deeply and touched her hair.

It had proved difficult to write the letter to this man, who she knew was her father although they had never met. It had taken courage and resolve. She might never even have learned the true facts if she had not found the small bundle of letters wrapped in red ribbon in her mother's dressing-table drawer after the funeral.

Catherine had read every word he had written.

A tear filled her eye as she looked at the bag beside her where she kept the letters. He had begged her mother to return in letter after letter. Year after year he had tried to get her to return to him and it was clear, even as his letters grew less frequent, that Nathan Berkley had loved his wife.

It was also clear from his words that Nathan Berkley had not been told of his daughter's existence. Catherine touched a lace handkerchief to her eyes and then returned her attention to the incredible, vast, rolling hills outside the carriage window. She thought about the letters. They had started out as notes of love and ended up being nothing more than words from a man with a broken heart.

She could tell what kind of man Nathan Berkley had been and, she hoped, still was. He wore his heart on his sleeve and it had been destroyed by a woman whom he had obviously been madly in love with. Catherine realized from his letters that none of them had ever been replied to and yet for some unknown reason her mother had kept them.

Why?

Had her mother loved him but buckled under the pressure of her wealthy relatives and disowned him? Was Nathan Berkley a man not considered good enough for a socialite?

Had her mother been so shallow?

Catherine sighed. She resolved that if he was still alive she would hold him in her arms and beg for forgiveness. Not for herself but for the actions of her heartless mother.

The beautiful young woman knew that the next stop would be the town of Deadlock, and there she would disembark. She had already wired ahead to reserve a room in a hotel. She prayed that all the stories she had heard about the Wild West were exaggerated and that she would not have any unwelcome problems with hot-blooded cowboys.

Catherine opened the bag and looked down into its silk-lined interior. On top of the bundle of ribbon-wrapped letters lay a twin-shot derringer.

That would be her only insurance.

She prayed that she would never be forced to use it.

7

The last rays of the sun ebbed as the fiery orb disappeared beyond the highest of the distant mountains. It was as though the heavens were alight for yet another end to yet another day. The big sky glowed like a raging wildfire above the Lazy B cattle spread. Yet none of the three cowboys who thundered across the vast ranges really noticed as they instinctively used the strange, eerie illumination to their advantage.

The intrepid horsemen just rode through the tall, sweet grass as they always did: fearlessly towards a distant goal that only one of their number knew anything about. As with all experienced cowboys they knew that nightfall always slowed their progress.

Appaloosa, Billy and Dobie realized that soon the heavenly fire would cease and stars would begin to fill the vast sky that loomed over them. Men who prized their horses as they did never pushed their horses as hard in the treacherous hours after sundown.

As always Appaloosa led his cowboys. His stallion ate up the ground beneath its hoofs vigorously as it fought against the skilled hands of its master who kept it in check. Both Billy and Dobie knew that at any time Appaloosa could relax his grip on his reins and his mighty horse would leave both their mounts to chew on its dust.

There were no faster mounts on the Lazy B Ranch than the small herd of appaloosas, which King had bred from the pair of handsome horses he had been given by the distant Nez Perce tribe years earlier. Neither of the cowboys who spurred hard just to keep close to King knew the real story of what their friend had done to be given such valuable mounts. It was well known that the distant tribe of Indians valued their spotted horses more than anything else. When they sold horses to other tribes they always ensured that the handsome creatures were gelded, yet they had given Appaloosa two healthy horses from which the cowboy had bred a string of offspring.

Whatever King had done for the noble Nez Perce it must have been something very special, the riders silently thought as they chased the powerful stallion. It must have been something that had set him apart from all other men.

The horses raced across the fertile range as the large moon suddenly appeared from behind a large, imposing dark cloud. The land before the three cowboys suddenly lit up as the eerie illumination cast its light across the ranch.

As they chased King both Dobie and Billy began to notice that he was not taking them on a direct course to the distant town of Deadlock. For some reason Appaloosa was leading them away from the trail to the town he had said they were heading for. They were not heading due north but north-east.

Hundreds of longhorn steers grazed the northern range as the trio of horsemen drove their mounts through the swaying grassland.

Moonlight danced along the lengths of their incredibly long, curved horns as the sturdy beasts watched the cowboys without interest. It was like riding through a herd of devils, but each of the cowboys was used to the strange sight. This was not the first time they had ridden at night, but it was the first time that the lead rider seemed to be so eager to reach his destination.

As his sturdy quarter horse thundered alongside his pal's mount in pursuit of King, Billy leaned across and stared at Dobie. 'Where do ya figure Appaloosa's headed, Dobie?'

'Damned if I know, Billy,' the younger cowboy yelled back. 'But this ain't the way to Deadlock.'

The two cowboys vainly spurred in an attempt to catch up with their leader, yet all they could do was watch the spotted rump of the magnificent stallion ahead of them and chase it into a dusty draw.

With every passing mile the pair of ranch hands knew they were getting further and further away from the trail they both knew was the shortest route to Deadlock.

Why was Appaloosa heading so far away from the trail? The question burned in the minds of the two trailing cowboys like a branding-iron.

Both thought they knew Appaloosa King better than they knew their own kinfolk, but both were wrong. There were many things about the lean horseman that nobody realized. Even though he had been very young when he had first drifted on to the Lazy B cattle spread, King had already crammed more adventure and danger into his short life than most men could have equalled in a dozen lifetimes.

He had the strange ability to excel at everything he undertook. He had not just learned to ride but had become an expert horseman. He had not just learned how to use a six-shooter but had become faster and more accurate with his pair of matched Colts than most gunfighters ever managed. Appaloosa King was a man it paid to befriend. Even though he was still shy of his thirtieth birthday he had the respect of his fellow cowboys and they knew that he would never allow any of them to attempt anything he was not willing to try himself.

After more than an hour the appaloosa stallion was brought to a sudden halt as it reached a shallow creek that snaked across the ground before them. The two cowboys reined in beside the tall horseman. Dust floated up into the moonlight.

King dismounted swiftly and allowed his mount to drop its neck and drink from the crystal-clear water.

'Get off them nags, boys,' he ordered. 'Water them horses and fill your canteens. We still got a long ride ahead of us.'

Both his companions did as he instructed. They held on to their reins and led their exhausted horses to drink from the fast-moving creek.

'Why are we heading to Deadlock, Appaloosa?' Dobie asked the tall King, who was studying the terrain before them with more than a little concern etched in his handsome features.

'We ain't,' King said in a low drawl. 'Leastways not straight away. We've got somewhere else to go first.'

Billy Smith forced the reins of his horse into Dobie's gloved hands and walked the distance between himself and King. He stepped in front of the ranch foreman and looked up into his eyes.

'I might be a few years younger than you, Appaloosa, but I'm way too old for riddles,' Billy said.

King nodded. 'You're right. I ought to be honest with both you and Dobie.'

'Then spill the beans, Appaloosa,' Billy pressed.

Dobie leaned over the neck of his

drinking horse. 'Has this got anything to do with that wire you had just before we saddled up, Appaloosa?'

Appaloosa again nodded. 'Give that man a cigar. Dobie. You ain't nowhere near as dumb as you look, boy.'

'Neither am I.' Billy moved even closer to King. 'What was in that telegram?'

King beat the dust off his hat against his chaps, then returned it to his dark hair. He tightened the drawstring under his chin and glanced down at the cowboy.

'It was a message from a varmint who reckoned he had news that I really needed to know about, Billy,' King explained.

'About what?'

'Rustlers.' King pulled the scrap of paper from his pocket and offered it to Billy. 'Read this.'

'You know I can't read, Appaloosa.' The cowboy shuffled his boots. 'I never had me no schooling. You read it.'

'OK. I'll read it then.' King turned

until the bright moon was over his shoulder. He screwed his eyes up and looked at the paper in his gloved hand. 'There is a gang of rustlers with sights on your steers. Come to Sidewinder Canyon by midnight and I'll tell you details. Bring $100.'

Billy watched as King folded the paper up and returned it to his pocket. 'You got any reason to figure on that wire being on the level, Appaloosa?'

King shrugged. 'I can't tell either way, Billy. The judge reckoned it was wise to find out, though.'

'Why are we heading to Deadlock?' Dobie piped up. 'Has that got to do with rustlers?'

Billy looked at his sleepy pal. 'Don't be dumb, Dobie. We got to pick up a package for the judge there. Besides, we ain't been heading towards Deadlock for more than an hour. You know that. Ain't that right, Appaloosa?'

King smiled at Billy. 'Yep. That's right.'

'Are we still going to have to pick up

a package for the judge or was that just horse feathers?' Billy raised his eyebrows.

'I sure hope it ain't heavy,' Dobie interrupted. 'I'm real tuckered. I broke me two mustangs yesterday and my bones are still loose.'

'It ain't that kinda package, Dobie,' King said.

Billy was about to walk back to his horse, then he paused and looked back at King. 'What kinda package are we gonna have to pick up, exactly?'

'A female type,' King replied as his stallion raised its head beside him.

'What?' Billy started to smile.

Dobie shook his head. 'Don't go telling me the judge has up and bought himself a mail-order wife.'

Billy removed his canteen from his saddle horn and unscrewed its stopper. 'The last thing the judge needs is a wife, Dobie.'

'Then who is this female?'

'The judge's daughter,' King told him.

Both cowboys grinned broadly.

'She's due to arrive in Deadlock in the next couple of days and we have to escort her safely back to the ranch, boys.' King stepped in his stirrup and boarded his high-shouldered mount. 'The judge don't want nothing harming her and that's why he's relying on us to make sure of that.'

Dobie's eyes widened. 'A real gal? Are you talking about a real, honest-to-goodness gal, Appaloosa? A grown-up type with all the curves in the right places?'

King gathered in his reins and nodded.

'Yep. A real, honest-to-goodness grown-up one.'

8

A black cauldron of fast-moving clouds cast their shadows across the moonlit terrain. It was as though a ghostly tidal wave was washing across the very land itself as the trio of deadly hired gunmen drove their horses towards the place they only knew from the markings on a map. Yet even though none of the well-armed riders had ever been to this desolate land that fringed the lush ranges of the Lazy B cattle spread, each of the Horton brothers felt as though he had travelled this path before.

The ground beneath the hoofs of their well-rested mounts echoed as they raced through a high-sided draw towards a distant mesa which, they knew, stood only a mile or so ahead of their destination.

They had made good time since they

had set out for the strangely named Sidewinder Canyon from Black River. They knew that men like Appaloosa King could never ignore telegraph messages when they hinted at the possibility of rustling. Even if the man whom they had tangled with years earlier did not believe there was any truth in the simple wire, he could never dismiss it.

King was not the kind of man who ever ignored warnings of any kind. He had a curiosity which had been the downfall of many of his kind. The notches on the brothers' lethal weaponry bore evidence of that. Curiosity did not always kill just the cat. Many men's enquiring minds had led them into the gun sights of the three Horton brothers.

Their horses increased their pace as the cold-blooded brothers drove on through the darkness of the draw and back out into the moonlight.

* * *

Earl Horton rode between his brothers with a confidence that had always been contagious to his siblings. As with all elder brothers, Earl inspired his kinfolk to believe that they could do whatever they desired to do. There was no man west of the Pecos who was immune to their deadly bullets.

His unflinching belief that they would always achieve their goal filled both his juniors with total conviction. Luke and Will rode beside Earl towards the strange, towering mesa bathed in the eerie light of the large moon. Both were filled with his infectious resolve.

This was going to be just another swift killing, like all those that had gone before. The three riders once again had the advantage, as they always had. They knew of their murderous intentions and King did not.

They had another advantage. This time they also knew their chosen prey. They knew his strengths and they also knew his weaknesses.

Appaloosa King would ride to the

canyon before midnight just as they had instructed him to do. Then they would bushwhack him.

It would be a turkey shoot.

The cowboy who had once proved to be a thorn in their sides would be hit by bullets from all sides of the canyon. This was going to be an execution that they each believed was long overdue.

As their horses thundered on past the towering mesa they spurred even harder. There was deathly eagerness in their souls. This was one killing which they all had dreamt of for years.

They could see their destination ahead of them through the unearthly moonlight. It looked exactly as the map had implied it would. With each stride of their powerful horses the brothers grew more and more confident.

To their left they could see the vast range of lush terrain that they knew was the famed Lazy B. To their right a few miles away from the moonlit canyon the beginnings of the great forest loomed.

Earl Horton balanced in his stirrups

and leaned back to slow his charging mount as his brothers copied his actions.

The closer the horsemen got the more they knew that they had been quite correct in their choice. Sidewinder Canyon was the perfect place for an execution. The three Horton brothers stopped their sturdy horses as they reached the narrow mouth of the moonlit canyon and allowed their dust to continue up into its shadowy heart.

Silently Earl noted that even if he had been able to design the perfect layout of a place to ambush their unsuspecting victim, he could not have bettered the one nature had created.

'There it is, boys,' the eldest of the Hortons announced with a sweep of his left arm. 'Just look at it. I never seen anywhere as perfect as that for laying a trap. It's made to order.'

The hired killers steadied their mounts and studied what lay before them with calculating eyes as Earl formulated a plan in his canny mind. In all his days he had never before seen anywhere that offered more cover for his brothers and himself from which to fire and was also devoid of anywhere for their target to hide from their lethal lead.

The canyon was no more than forty feet wide and had high walls to either side. The floor of the canyon was virtually flat with no fallen boulders large enough for a man to seek refuge behind. To both sides the top of the canyon was rugged and marked by huge rocks which were bigger than any of their horses.

'This must have been built by the Devil himself,' Will chuckled.

Luke Horton grinned. 'Damn right. This is gonna be even easier than we reckoned.'

The eldest of the brothers silently noted that there were trails to either side, which led up to the top of the mesa. He nodded.

'Perfect,' Earl Horton pronounced.

He pulled a cigar from the silver case and bit off the tip of the long dark smoke. 'This is just like the map indicated, boys.'

'It looks like this place was made for bushwhacking.' Luke nodded and watched as his elder brother struck a match and raised it to the end of the cigar. As smoke billowed from his mouth Earl pointed to both sides.

'You're right, Luke,' Earl agreed. He pointed his cigar upward. 'I figure you can head up to that side, Will. I'll ride up to the other side. We can nestle down with our Winchesters to crossfire from both directions whilst you head on up the canyon and lie on your belly, Luke. Use the shadows so he can't see you but you can see him.'

'We'll cut the critter to ribbons.' Luke gloated and laughed out loud.

'This ain't gonna be just a killing,' Will chuckled. 'This is gonna be a slaughter.'

'Ain't no more than Appaloosa King

deserves.' Earl sucked on his cigar and allowed the smoke to drift from between his teeth. 'That cowboy cost us a pretty penny a few years back by interfering in our business. It's about time that bastard was made to pay for that. Right?'

His brothers nodded.

The eldest of the brothers reached inside his coat and pulled out a gold hunter watch from his vest pocket. He opened its lid. He allowed the moonlight to shine on its dial before snapping it shut again.

'It's thirty minutes after eleven,' Earl announced, returning the watch to his vest. He slid his silver-plated Winchester from its saddle scabbard. An unholy grin wreathed his features as he looked at the weapon. 'We've got half an hour to get into position.'

'Plenty of time,' Will said.

Luke leaned over his mount's neck. 'I'll ride up the canyon and belly down.'

Earl nodded. He watched Luke spur and gallop up the narrow, shadow-filled canyon. Then he turned to his younger brother.

'You ride up there and find yourself a real big rock to hide behind,' he instructed. 'I want Appaloosa King to taste our lead from all sides, Will. This'll be a turkey shoot.'

'I can't wait to get him in my sights.' Will touched his hat brim, turned his horse and rode to the side of the canyon wall. He spurred hard and drove his mount up the dusty trail which led up to the top of the canyon.

'This is gonna be so damn sweet.' Earl rested the repeating rifle across his lap, eased his own horse around and headed to the opposite side of the canyon. He tossed his long black cigar aside and encouraged his mount up the sandy incline.

The higher Earl Horton got as he rode up the steep incline the better his view of the vast terrain became. His eyes screwed up as they focused on the cloud of hoof dust far off in the distance. He knew the cowboy he had been hired to kill had swallowed the bait and was approaching Sidewinder Canyon at pace.

His horse continued up the steep incline as its master looked all around the vast, moonlit terrain surrounding the rugged outcrop of rocks. He tapped his spurs; then to his left he saw something that made him ease his reins back.

Earl Horton turned on his saddle and gazed out towards the very edge of the forest, which he knew was filled with untold numbers of Indians. Dust rose from around the hoofs of his stationary stallion into the cold air.

It was a horseman.

A solitary rider sat upon a beautiful tall horse that put his own nag to shame. Even at distance Earl could see that it was a black horse that seemed to gleam in the light of the moon. But it was no ordinary black animal beneath the horseman, for this horse had a silver mane and tail which moved like the waves on a beach as the night breeze caught them.

In all his days Earl Horton had never seen or even heard of any living horses like that, but he had heard tales of a mythical horseman who rode such an animal.

For the first time in his sordid life Earl Horton was afraid and he did not understand why.

Was he actually looking down at the legendary Skyhorse?

Legend had it that Skyhorse was an avenging angel who sought out evil and destroyed all those who perpetrated it. Earl had heard these stories since he and his brothers had first ventured west.

'You're being loco,' Earl told himself. He gripped his reins and then tapped his spurs again. His mount started up the trail again as the deadly hired gunman kept watching the strange figure, which was obviously looking back at him. The mist from the forest curled like a herd of phantoms and danced around the statuesque horse and its master.

It was an unnerving sight even for a man who made his living by killing for money. Few men had ever dared to face down any of the Hortons, but the horseman did not appear to be impressed by what he was studying.

A cold chill traced the eldest Horton's spine. It had nothing to do with the temperature. As the tall horse reached the very top of the canyon wall Earl rubbed his eyes and gazed down at the rider again.

Whoever it was, he was sure interested in him, Earl thought. Earl dismounted and led his horse to a large boulder and secured his long leathers to it. He tightened the knot and straightened up.

Then he noticed that the horseman was gone. Only the unholy mist remained.

A sudden dread filled his innards. Earl looked all around the land that lay far below him. It was a vast land of contrasts. There was definitely something about the look of the horseman that had troubled the normally cold-blooded hired gunman. Had he seen something that did not belong in the world of living creatures?

Had he seen Skyhorse?

Or had he just seen an ordinary rider who had emerged from the forest? Then a dozen unanswerable questions filled his mind.

Who was that horseman?

Where had he gone?

Had he turned his mount and gone back into the forest?

Had he spurred and ridden into the black shadows that stretched out across the range towards the canyon?

Was he coming towards Earl and his brothers?

If so, why? Who or what was he?

The only thing Earl knew for sure was that it had not been Appaloosa King. That cowboy rode horses that were unique in these parts and were nothing like the horse that had so amazed him.

Earl Horton opened his cigar case, removed a smoke and bit off its tip. He spat at the ground, then struck a match along his rifle barrel. He cupped the flame and inhaled the smoke deep into his lungs. Again he thought about the horseman. He had not looked like an Indian, but it was hard to tell in the strange half-light created by the huge moon above him. Earl tried to dismiss the rider from his thoughts and concentrate on the job at hand.

He was here for only one reason.

To kill Appaloosa King.

He cradled the silver-plated rifle in his hands and made his way to the very edge of the high precipice. He knelt and pushed the hand guard down. A brass casing was expelled from the Winchester's magazine as Earl dropped down beside a smooth boulder.

With curling smoke trailing from the cigar gripped in his teeth, Earl pulled the brim of his hat down and stared back out in the direction of the Lazy B cattle spread. Yet no matter how hard the lethal assassin tried he could not get the sight of the horseman out of his thoughts.

There was another part of the legend which gnawed at him as he narrowed his eyes and stared out to where he could see the fast-approaching hoof dust out in the direction of the Lazy B.

It was said that anyone with evil in their blackened hearts who happened to set eyes on Skyhorse was doomed to die at his hands.

Earl swallowed hard and stared at the advancing dust.

'Hurry up, Appaloosa. I don't like this damn place,' he whispered.

9

A hundred or more longhorn steers separated as Appaloosa King rode alongside his two fellow cowboys through the swaying moonlit grass towards the high mesa and the canyon beyond. The lead rider abruptly drew rein and stopped his high-shouldered stallion. Both Billy and Dobie dragged their own mounts to a halt next to the tall, slim rider.

They watched as Appaloosa raised himself off his saddle and balanced in his stirrups. The lean horseman stared ahead of them like an eagle in cold silence.

'What you looking at, Appaloosa?' Dobie wearily asked.

Billy tapped his spurs against the sides of his quarter horse and steered the horse next to the silent King. He looked up, then scratched his chin.

'Are you looking for the varmint who sent you that telegraph, Appaloosa?' he asked.

The ranch foreman lowered himself and sighed.

'Something caught my eye up there,' Appaloosa said.

'What?' Dobie queried.

'Yeah,' Billy wondered. 'What caught your eye?'

Appaloosa glanced at both men. 'That I ain't too sure about. Might have been a trick of the light but on the other hand it might have been something else.'

Dobie exhaled and pulled his collar up to protect his neck from the night air. 'It might be the critter that sent you the message, Appaloosa.'

King shook his head. 'I'm starting to have grave doubts about that damn wire, boys. Seems like a damn good place for us to get shot at.'

'Who'd wanna shoot at us?' Billy said with a grin.

'We're just cowboys,' Dobie added.

'We're Lazy B cowboys. There's a whole heap of folks who don't like the fact that Judge Berkley has the best longhorn herd in these parts,' King said thoughtfully. 'We've had a lot of ranch hands killed over the years. There's always somebody who's willing to kill.'

Both Billy and Dobie suddenly turned their heads and squinted into the eerie light over the land that lay before them.

'I might be being a tad cautious but I don't hanker after riding into no ambush, boys.' Appaloosa leaned back, unbuckled one of his saddle-bag satchels and pulled out a pair of binoculars. He rubbed their lenses with the tails of his bandanna.

Dobie smiled. 'You don't want us getting hurt. Right, Appaloosa?'

King raised the binoculars to his eyes. 'I don't give a damn about you. I'm worried my horse will get hurt.'

Dobie looked at Billy. 'He's joshing.'

'Is he?' Billy shrugged.

King adjusted the focus wheel on

the binoculars. 'Something caught the moonlight up there on the top of the canyon wall.'

'Do you see anything?' Billy asked.

King exhaled loudly as he searched the moonlit crags. He moved the powerful binoculars from side to side as he searched the tops of both sides of the canyon for any hint of movement.

'Do you see anyone?' Dobie pressed nervously.

Appaloosa lowered the glasses. 'Nope, but I'm sure I saw something get caught in the light of that big old moon.'

'It could have been an owl or maybe a vulture,' Billy reasoned. 'There's plenty of mighty big birds in these parts, Appaloosa.'

Appaloosa shook his head and hung the binoculars from his saddle horn. 'Maybe it was a big old bird but it sure didn't look like one to me. What I saw was a flash like when the sun catches a mirror or the like.'

Dobie stood in his stirrups and

pointed over the tall, swaying grass between them and their destination at the high wall of the canyon. 'You mean like that, Appaloosa?'

Billy pushed his hat brim up and squinted. 'What in tarnation is that?'

King glanced up to where Dobie was aiming his gloved finger. His attention was drawn to a brief series of flashes emanating from the jagged crags, as though there were a glistening jewel in the darkness. The ranch foreman swiftly grabbed the binoculars once again. He brought them to his eyes and stared up at the canyon walls.

'I knew it,' King said.

'What do you see, Appaloosa?' Billy asked.

'I see a varmint with a rifle, Billy,' King replied as he again lowered his glasses. 'A silver-plated rifle.'

Dobie accepted the binoculars and looked up to where he had seen the flashes of light dance off the repeating rifle.

'I see him, Appaloosa. He's buckled

down real good but that fancy carbine of his is catching the moonlight,' Dobie said.

'Hand me them spyglasses, Dobie,' Billy urged.

Dobie handed the binoculars to the cowboy and then returned his attention to King. The ranch foreman looked troubled as he continued to stare ahead.

'What's wrong, Appaloosa?'

'That ain't no informer ready to spill the beans about a bunch of rustlers, boys,' King muttered firmly as he beat a gloved fist on to the top of his saddle horn. 'That critter is waiting up there to pick me off. That telegraph was just to lure me out here to shoot me.'

'Why?'

'We all got us enemies, Dobie.' King sighed as his mind began to race. 'Reckon I've ruffled more than a few feathers in my time. It only takes one critter with a grudge and a well-oiled gun to take it in his mind to get even.'

'I don't know of anyone with a fancy

silver carbine, Appaloosa,' Dobie said.

'Me neither.' Billy shrugged.

'Maybe that varmint is a hired gun,' King ventured. 'Some folks are too yella to do their own killing. That bush-whacker might have been paid to snuff out my candle.'

Dobie and Billy looked at one another. Neither spoke.

Appaloosa turned on his saddle and looked at the longhorned steers which were spread out all around them in the ocean of tall, sweet grass.

'I got me an idea,' Appaloosa said. 'Do you boys want to help me round up these longhorns?'

'What for?' Billy wondered.

King smiled. 'I figure that rifleman might find it a tad difficult to pick me off if I'm riding in the middle of a herd of stampeding steers.'

Billy reached across and grabbed King's sleeve. 'I ain't gonna let you ride towards that bastard on your own, Appaloosa. I'm tagging along with you.'

'So am I.' Dobie nodded.

Appaloosa King inhaled deeply. 'It'll be dangerous. It might even be fatal.'

'We're cowboys, Appaloosa.' Billy turned his horse and studied the steers scattered around them. 'It's all part of the job.'

King nodded and tapped his spurs. 'C'mon. Let's round up some of these fat old steers.'

10

It was a long while after midnight and Earl Horton was beginning to get nervous as he adjusted himself for the umpteenth time behind the huge rock as he perched on the lip of the canyon. He looked back at his mount, which was also starting to get edgy behind him. His eyes squinted across the canyon to where his brother Will was kneeling above a high precipice. Then he looked down and along the narrow floor of the canyon to where Luke lay in wait. His left hand searched for and found his golden hunter. He flicked its lid open.

It was nearly 12.30.

'Where the hell are you, Appaloosa?' Earl growled to himself as he dropped the pocket watch back into his pocket and resumed his grip on the barrel of his silver-plated rifle. 'I saw your damn dust an hour ago. You should have been here by now.'

Then another more fearful thought filled his mind. It was the irrational memory of the mysterious rider on the strange horse. Earl was becoming convinced that the rider was somewhere in the canyon range. The cold night air chewed into the marrow of the ambusher's bones. Why had he and his brothers been made to wait so long for Appaloosa King to make his appearance? Every extra minute was torturous as the air grew colder and the night progressed.

Earl could not remain kneeling beside the frost-covered rock a moment longer, he thought. He was stiffening up and could no longer feel his feet. He forced himself back up on to his boots.

The eldest of the deadly trio of brothers moved away from his hiding-place and carefully negotiated his way across the jagged icy rocks. He clambered closer to the very edge of the canyon, then rested, his hands clutching on to his Winchester.

'Come on, Appaloosa,' he mumbled. 'I'm getting my rump frozen off up here. Where are you?'

The words had barely left the hired killer's throat when his attention was dragged to his brother perched across the other side of the canyon. Earl Horton's head turned and his eyes narrowed as he focused on the waving arm of his sibling.

Earl placed a hand to the side of his mouth and shouted out across the narrow distance between them.

'What, Will? What's got you all fired up, boy?'

The youngest of the deadly clan pointed urgently with his rifle out into the range to where the towering mesa loomed.

'Look, Earl. What the hell is that?' Will screamed back.

The most brutal of the Horton brothers crawled across the boulders and stared from the lip of the perilous top of the jagged canyon out into the eerie moonlit range. For a moment he could not see anything, but then he noticed the cloud of dust that billowed from the base of the mesa.

'That's more than one rider making all that dust,' Earl muttered as his eyes strained to see.

'What is it, Earl?' Will Horton yelled out again as he too fearfully tried to work out what was headed in their direction.

The cloud of dust was billowing up into the frosty air above the range. It sparkled like a million fireflies as it danced in the moonlight. It looked as though a bomb had exploded some-where out on the range and its wrath was coming to engulf them.

Utterly confused, Earl rubbed his tired eyes. He was about to call back to his troubled sibling when he began to hear the distinctive sound of angry steers. Longhorns made a unique sound when bellowing, which could freeze the blood of even the most courageous of souls.

'Holy smoke,' he muttered to himself. He straightened up. 'I got me a real bad feeling that's a stampeding herd of longhorns.'

Will Horton moved to the very edge of the rocks upon which he was standing. Loose grit fell from under his boots down into the blackness below as the hired assassin called out to his brother again.

'Is that a bunch of steers, Earl?'

'Damn right, Will,' Earl yelled back.

'What made them stampede?'

'Not what,' Earl shouted. 'Who? That's gotta be the work of Appaloosa.'

Then the eldest of the brothers suddenly realized that he was right. He and Will were not simply witnessing a herd of massive longhorns randomly racing across the range of tall grass. There were cowboys expertly driving them towards the mouth of the canyon. Through the dense clouds of dust he could see ropes being swung towards the back of the herd.

A terrible realization filled Earl

Horton with dread. It gripped him with fear. He knew that if the herd of stampeding longhorns were driven into the narrow canyon they would run roughshod over his brother. There was nowhere to take cover in the confines of the canyon. No safe haven or sanctuary from the brutal hoofs of the powerful beasts which were going to be funnelled into Sidewinder Canyon.

If Luke Horton remained where he was he would be trampled to death. Earl swung around and stared down into the canyon where he had sent Luke an hour earlier. Somewhere in the dark shadows Luke was totally unaware of what was approaching. Earl hopped across the uneven rocks, raised a hand to his face and shouted.

'Luke! Luke! Get out of there, Luke!' Earl yelled down into the abyss. There was no reply. 'Why don't he reply, Will?'

Will teetered on the rim of the canyon opposite his brother, tugged his reins free and pulled his horse closer to him. 'I bet that idiot has fallen asleep,

Earl. You know what he's like.'

'Yeah, you might be right.' Earl looked across at the range. The cloud of hoof dust was looming as the longhorns got closer and closer. 'If he is asleep we have to wake the damn fool up before that herd enters the canyon.'

Will's head moved back and forth from his elder sibling to the terrifying cloud which was filled with snorting steers being driven towards them. 'Them longhorns are awful close, Earl. Too damn close for comfort. We gotta stop them.'

'We gotta try,' Earl corrected. He raised the Winchester to his shoulder. He closed one eye, stared along the gleaming barrel, then squeezed the rifle's trigger. The canyon rocked with the deafening reverberations of the shot.

A plume of fiery venom spewed from the barrel. The herd of longhorns continued towards the canyon. The eldest of the Horton brothers repeated his action over and over again until the air was filled with choking rifle smoke.

He had seen one of the burly steers drop, but the others kept on coming. It seemed that even lethal lead could not stop the stampeding cattle. They were more fearful of the cowboys who drove them than the bullets that had come down from the towering top of the canyon. Nothing could stop them.

'Damn it all,' Earl cursed. He narrowed his eyes and stared into the cloud of dust, which now engulfed the star-filled heavens. Then he looked to his brother. 'C'mon, Will. We have to get down there and try to reach Luke before them damn beeves do.'

The younger brother signalled his agreement as Earl carefully made his way across the jagged rocks back to where his horse was tethered.

Will grabbed the horn of his saddle, thrust his boot into his stirrup and mounted his horse in one swift action. The youngest of the hired killers tapped his spurs and steered the animal down through the moonlight towards the mouth of the canyon. As his mount negotiated the treacherous trail Will glanced across and saw Earl throw himself on to his own horse and start his descent.

Both horsemen kept one eye on the approaching steers and another on the perilous path their horses were carefully descending.

Time was running short and both the Horton brothers knew it. They not only had to try and reach the canyon floor as quickly as possible but also ensure that their mounts did not make a false step.

The sound of pounding hoofs and snorting steers began to echo off the walls of the canyon as the longhorns thundered closer to the canyon. It was the sound of certain death approaching at speed and both of the Hortons knew their own devilish plan to murder Appaloosa King had somehow been turned on its head.

Now they were the ones in mortal danger. There was no time to lose: a single mistake could prove fatal.

Both brothers retraced the route they had taken to reach the top of the canyon and leaned back against their saddle cantles as their horses scrambled down the soft ground towards the range.

There was desperation now in their heartless souls. They realized that there was not a second to spare. The ominous cloud of dust rose like an unearthly monster from the high, swaying grass as the hoofs of the massive beasts ripped up the ground. They could see the horns of the huge steers catching the eerie light of the moon as more than a dozen of the animals crashed through the high grass.

Then even more snorting longhorns followed.

The noise of the charging steers was deafening. No speeding locomotive at full throttle could have equalled the chilling sound of the muscular herd as they were driven on towards the canyon.

Now there was only open range

between the mouth of the canyon and the approaching steers.

Earl and Will reached the floor of the canyon at the same moment. Both horses staggered as their masters dragged rein and turned them towards the long, shadow-filled canyon. The hired killers feverishly lashed their mounts' tails with the long barrels of their repeating rifles.

With terror gripping their innards both of the Horton brothers spurred and thundered into the depths of the black canyon. Neither of the horsemen could see their brother as they rode through the shadow-filled canyon. Again they both called out, but for some reason Luke did not answer.

Will drew his galloping mount close to his brother's and yelled out.

'Where the hell is he?'

Earl shook his head. He had no answer.

11

A myriad stars vainly attempted to compete with the large moon which hung directly above the high mesa. Yet even the moon could not compete with the billowing clouds of hoof dust that rose above the pounding beasts. Its light was nearly obliterated as the steers charged ahead from the cowboys who had rounded them up.

Appaloosa King balanced in his stirrups as his trusty stallion forged on. The intrepid horseman looked back. He had instructed both his followers not to trail him beyond the mesa but the two cowboys had ignored King. They did not intend to allow him to face the unknown assassin alone.

That was not the Lazy B way. They stuck together no matter how danger-ous the odds might be. They had heard the rifle fire and the sickening bellow of the steer who had been cut down by one of the bushwhackers' bullets.

Neither cowboy slowed his pace.

Billy and Dobie rode around the stricken longhorn in their pursuit of Appaloosa King. They were swinging their cutting ropes to ensure that none of the steers slowed its pace whilst Appaloosa valiantly rode his magnificent stallion through the middle of the thundering herd.

No tornado could have created more dust or sounded quite as terrifying as the small herd of wide-eyed longhorns did. They had been rounded up by the cowboys and forced towards the canyon with expert ease.

Dust filled the night air as King leaned over the neck of his thundering stallion and rode in the very middle of the stampeding steers. The horseman knew that if his fearless mount took one false step he would be brought down and crushed to death beneath their unforgiving hoofs, yet Appaloosa kept riding to where he knew the rifleman he had spotted an hour earlier was waiting.

The longhorns had carved a wide path through the lush swaying grass, but now there was nothing but open range ahead of them.

Appaloosa King wondered whether the man with the silver Winchester could see him from his high vantage point, because he could not see anything except the powerful bodies of the steers, which surrounded his horse.

The rifle fire had been short and sweet and then had stopped for some reason Appaloosa had yet to understand. He gritted his teeth and screwed up his dust-caked eyes as he trailed the steers ahead of him. He tried to see if the rifleman was still on the top of the high canyon walls, but it was impossible.

There was too much dust filling the moonlit air to see anything clearly, but Appaloosa King knew that the dust was his only shield. If he could not see the canyon then it was doubtful whether the rifleman could see him.

He spurred and clung on to his reins as the stallion kept pace with the beasts. He knew that there was only a quarter-mile of rough range between the high mesa and Sidewinder Canyon. He was getting closer with each beat of his young heart.

Again Appaloosa looked over his shoulder to where his pals were riding. Billy and Dobie were still within spitting distance. He swung around, looked ahead and thought about the unknown sniper with the silver Winchester.

Would he be able to get the drop on the bushwhacker before the repeating rifle spewed out more lead? The troublesome thought filled his mind. He knew there was no room for error.

This was the biggest gamble of his life.

If it paid off Appaloosa King would be able to get his hands on the rifleman who had lured him to the remote canyon and then discover whether he was an old enemy or someone who had been hired to kill him.

The dust began to clear. Appaloosa King rose high in his stirrups and started to drive his powerful mount between the charging longhorns.

'Come on, Moon boy,' the cowboy urged his mount.

With masterful skill the horseman left the herd trailing in his wake and steered towards the moonlit rocks. It did not take long for the appaloosa stallion to reach the ancient wall of rocks.

The Lazy B foreman was about to spur and ride up the steep incline to where he had earlier spotted the deadly Earl Horton when he noticed the telltale dust hanging in the icy night air at the mouth of the canyon.

King leaned far to his left and guided the galloping stallion towards the entrance to the canyon. The closer he rode to the natural fissure the more his keen instincts noticed that the rifleman had not been alone.

Two sets of hoof-tracks merged and

then went up into the canyon. Appaloosa steadied the snorting stallion for a few moments as the herd of steers behind him came closer.

His keen eyes studied the churned-up sand, which stretched out before him. The light of the moon had still not found the canyon. It was bathed in total darkness but for some reason the pair of bushwhackers had ridden down from the relative safety of the high rocks and headed into it.

The cowboy knew he would not find the answers to any of his questions unless he too entered Sidewinder Canyon.

With no thought for his own safety, Appaloosa King spurred.

12

Luke Horton had ridden far further into the canyon than either of his brothers had realized. They rode shoulder by shoulder until they came to a bend. The rocks far above them were jagged and a shaft of eerie moonlight managed to reach the canyon floor.

Their brother's horse was the first thing they saw as they slowed their mounts. Then the youngest of the Hortons spotted a shape to their right.

'There he is, Earl,' Will said. He dragged his reins up to his chest and slowed his horse. 'I don't get it. How come he ain't moving?'

A sudden dread filled Earl Horton. He leaned back in his saddle and stopped his horse in its tracks. In the hired killer's mind there were only two reasons why a man would be lying on frosty ground, not moving a muscle.

Sleep or death; Luke did not look asleep to his elder brother.

Both horsemen dismounted quickly. They moved towards their brother. Earl knelt and checked the motionless figure.

'Is it Luke?' Will asked.

'Yeah, it's Luke,' Earl answered.

'Wake up, Luke,' Will urged as he heard the sound of distant pounding hoofs coming up the canyon towards them. 'We gotta get out of here.'

'He's dead, Will.' Earl rolled the limp body over on to its back and stared at his brother's face. It was twisted and barely recognizable.

Will leaned over in total shock. 'What? He can't be dead, Earl. How can he be dead?'

Earl returned to his full height. 'Damned if I know, Will boy. We didn't hear any shots and I couldn't find any blood.'

Suddenly both the brothers heard the unmistakable sound of a rattler coming from the shadows behind Luke's dead body. As fast as the blink of an eye Earl drew one of his six-shooters, cocked its hammer and fired at the lethal serpent.

The bullet ripped the snake's head from its body. It fell limply across Luke's legs.

'A rattler!' Will gasped.

'Reckon we now know how this canyon got its name, Will,' Earl said as he slid his smoking gun back into its holster. 'It must have bit Luke when he lay down. By the look on his face it must have been a real bad way to die.'

Will shook his head. 'Where we gonna bury him, Earl?'

The eldest of the Hortons grabbed his reins, stepped into his stirrup and mounted. 'We ain't. Come on. We have to ride.'

Will grabbed his saddle horn and swung up on to his saddle. He poked both boots into his stirrups and gathered up his reins.

'We're gonna leave him here for buzzard bait?'

Earl narrowed his eyes. 'Listen. Hear

that? I hear someone heading this way. By my reckoning that has to be Appaloosa. I can also hear those steers. They'll be on us at any moment. We have to ride.'

'What about Luke?' Will asked.

Earl grabbed his brother's bandanna and tightened it hard until their eyes met. 'He's dead, Will. Get that into your damn head. We can't help Luke and if we don't get out of here real fast, we'll be dead as well. Savvy?'

Reluctantly the younger Horton nodded. 'I savvy.'

Earl turned his horse. 'Come on.'

'Where are you headed?'

'Any place away from here, Will.'

Both horsemen spurred. They had barely ridden a quarter of a mile along the canyon when Earl noticed a gully in the side of the otherwise solid rocks.

'There.' Earl pointed. 'Follow me.'

Both horsemen took cover in the gully. They turned their mounts and faced the canyon. The sound of thundering hoofs grew louder.

'What we gonna do, Earl?'

Earl glanced at his brother, drew one of his guns and cocked its hammer. 'Hell. We're gonna do what we were paid to do, Will boy. We're gonna kill Appaloosa King.'

13

Knowing that the two unknown riders might be waiting for him anywhere along the narrow canyon did not deter the fearless horseman. He did not slow his pace as he continued to ride through the blackest of shadows deeper into the canyon than he had ever gone before. Sidewinder Canyon was a place into which it was not wise to venture, especially at night. As its name implied, it was reputed to be filled with the most venomous of rattlesnakes. Throughout all his years upon the nearby Lazy B cattle spread King had only entered the canyon when in search of stray steers. Usually it had proved a futile venture, as he had never once found any of Judge Berkley's famed longhorns alive in the eerie canyon.

The ranch foreman knew that there had to be a great many of the poisonous snakes nestling in the rugged rocks through which he was travelling, but as long as he kept his mount at full gallop he imagined he was safe. Yet the most optimistic soul would have grave doubts that even riding at pace was enough to prevent the fangs of a lethal sidewinder striking out from the darkness.

Concern about being cut down by an ambusher's cowardly bullets could not compete with the thought of his precious horse being bitten by a deadly rattler. After what had seemed like an eternity to the courageous horseman there was a challenger to the dark shadows.

The moon was starting to clear the highest point of the jagged canyon rim, far above the charging stallion. More and more shafts of eerie light shone down into the narrow confines. The shadows were under attack from the bright heavenly orb and for a few brief hours there would only be one victor.

As the appaloosa stallion thundered into the moonlight its master rose in his stirrups and stared ahead at the unexpected sight that confronted him. He had heard a gunshot only a few minutes earlier. As he set eyes upon the dead body ahead of him he supposed that one of the riders he was pursuing had killed the other.

Appaloosa slowed his mount with one hand as his other rested on his holstered gun grip. The stallion slowed as it neared the swollen body of Luke Horton. He stopped the horse and stared down at it. The moonlight revealed the truth. Even without seeing the twin puncture holes of the rattler's fangs Appaloosa knew exactly what fate had sent the dead man to his Maker. The victims of sidewinder bites had a certain look about them.

It was a sight branded into his memory for all time.

He steadied his horse and looked all around him. There were dozens of snakes moving into the light of the moon, as if to feed off its strange illumination. Appaloosa felt a chill trace his spine. Then he heard the sound that he had all but forgotten about.

It was sound of the herd of longhorns. The cowboy looked back over his shoulder and suddenly realized that they filled the narrow canyon from one side to the other.

Their bellowing moans echoed off the rocky walls as if warning anything in their path to find cover. But there was no cover.

There was nowhere to hide.

Appaloosa swung the stallion full circle as the horror of his situation dawned on him.

He had blindly followed two sets of hoof tracks to this spot and their trail led away from the body. Then he saw Luke Horton's mount across the canyon. This body was neither of the riders he had trailed. This was someone else.

He ran a gloved hand along the neck of the snorting stallion and desperately tried to think of a way out of the mess he had got himself into.

'Easy, Moon,' Appaloosa said. He looked up the canyon ahead of him. It was a place utterly unknown to him, but it was the only option left open to him.

The anxious young cowboy looked back again. The sound of the approaching herd was now deafening. It had already dawned on Appaloosa that he had made a really bad mistake by trailing the riders. It was now far too late to retreat.

He could not head back to the range without being trampled to death by his own steers; if he continued on he was riding to where the bushwhacker and his cohort were.

Either way his chances were slim.

'Damn it all. Reckon we're in a whole heap of trouble, Moon,' the cowboy cursed. He swung his faithful mount round as he again saw the snakes, which were closing in on his horse's legs. 'We've gotta get out of here fast.'

Then the longhorns burst through the shadows and charged towards him.

Appaloosa gripped his reins firmly.

'No more time for thinking, boy. Come on, Moon.'

Appaloosa whipped the tail of the stallion with his long leathers and drove the animal away from the approaching steers.

The horse obeyed its master.

Like a bullet shooting from the barrel of a gun the stallion galloped up the canyon.

Then another sound filled the air.

It was the sound of bullets.

As the startled cowboy turned to see where the shots were coming from he felt the impact as a bullet hit him. No mule kick could have felt so powerful.

It took every scrap of the cowboy's skill to remain atop his galloping mount. Appaloosa buckled in agony and held on grimly for dear life.

'Keep going, Moon boy,' he gasped as more shots rang out behind him. 'Keep going.'

14

Moonlight shone briefly upon a spurt of crimson gore as from the narrow crag in the canyon wall both the Horton brothers looked through the acrid gunsmoke at the fleeing horseman. Earl sat astride his mount and felt the ground beneath his horse's hoofs tremble as the longhorns drew closer to the brothers' hiding place. He shook the spent casings from his six-shooter, plucked fresh bullets from his gunbelt and slid them into the smoking chambers of the weapon.

He glanced at his younger brother, who had already reloaded his own .45.

'We got him, Earl,' Will said. He cocked the hammer of his gun and rammed his spurs into his mount. 'C'mon. We can finish the bastard.'

The elder brother watched in horror as Will encouraged his mount out into the canyon and prepared to set off after the wounded Appaloosa King.

'What the hell are you doing, Will?' Earl yelled out. 'Get back here.'

The sound of the approaching steers was now deafening. The entire canyon shook as Will turned his horse in readiness to chase the wounded Appaloosa.

Suddenly the massive longhorns appeared before the open-mouthed Earl Horton. It was unlike anything the hired killer had ever witnessed. Even the choking dust could not hide the horrific sight from his unblinking eyes.

For one second Will was there, the next he had vanished beneath the hoofs of the stampeding steers. Earl leaned back and tried to think but his brain had been numbed by the sight of his brother vanishing under the powerful beasts.

Then the steers were gone. Only their dust remained in the unholy moonlight. It lingered and mocked the onlooker as he focused on the bloodstained sand before him.

Earl could not take his eyes from the sand. There were chunks of his brother scattered for as far as he could see. It looked as though Will had been not only crushed but shredded into unrecognizable fragments. Earl tilted his head and tried to comprehend how a man could be reduced to mere stains on moonlit sand.

Even the horse had been trampled to death and had its limbs broken into pulp.

'You young fool,' Earl whispered as his hands toyed with the smoking gun in his hands. 'Didn't you hear the cattle coming, boy?'

He was about to spur his own skittish mount when he heard the pounding of horses' hoofs approaching. His eyes screwed up and a rage erupted inside his blackened soul.

He cocked his gun hammer and waited.

The deadly assassin did not have to wait long.

Billy and Dobie rode through the

unearthly moonlight and passed the horrific remains of the youngest of his brothers. Earl watched, then urged his mount out of the gully. He turned the tall horse and stared at the backs of the two Lazy B cowboys.

He did not call out to them. Earl Horton had no desire to see the faces of the cowboys who had driven the muscular longhorns into the narrow canyon.

All he wanted to do was make them pay.

Faster than the blink of an eye Earl fanned his gun hammer and blasted all six bullets into the backs of the cowboys. His aim was as deadly as ever. Both Billy and Dobie were lifted off their saddles. Their arms floated in the air as they tumbled to the ground.

As the smoke trailed upwards from his gun barrel Earl Horton gritted his teeth and swiftly reloaded his Colt. He stared at his handiwork with cold eyes. The back-shooter then gritted his teeth and rammed the weapon into its holster. Even the thick leather holster could not prevent the heat of the weapon from warming his thigh.

'How come you never die easy, Appaloosa?' Earl growled to himself. 'I've killed dozens of critters in my time but you always manage to cheat death. This time will be different, though. This time you're gonna pay top dollar for me losing my brothers. I'll chase you all the way to Hell if need be. There ain't nowhere to hide.'

The sound of the rampaging longhorns grew fainter as they continued along the canyon. The pitiless killer dragged his silver-barrelled Winchester from its scabbard and forced fresh bullets into its magazine as his vengeful mind festered and brooded upon how he would punish the already wounded cowboy.

As the embittered horseman leaned back and slid the primed carbine back into its hand-tooled saddle case he heard something far above him. Earl kicked the side of his tall mount and the animal turned until its master was facing the wall of rock that loomed over him. Fragments of dust and small rocks fell down through the moonlight towards the hired gunman. He pulled on his reins and the stallion stepped back until the rider was able to see the top of the jagged rocks.

To his amazement Earl Horton was looking up at the very same horseman he had seen more than an hour before, close by the forest. All he knew for sure was that the strange horseman was now much nearer. Horton focused hard. There was something unearthly about the rider.

'Skyhorse,' Earl muttered under his breath.

He had no inkling how long the silent rider had been there or how much he had witnessed. Sweat ran down from his hatband and burned his eyes but he refused to blink, for to do so would give the strange vision a chance to vanish as he had done earlier.

'Damn it all! Are you Skyhorse?'

Horton screamed up at the horseman as he drew his six-shooter. He clawed back its hammer until it fully locked. 'Are you? Answer me.'

There was no reply.

Earl Horton was about to fire his .45 when the magnificent black stallion with the silver mane and tail reared up and pawed at the frosty air. Horton squeezed his trigger and sent a deafening red-hot taper of lethal lead up at the defiant horse and rider. It was like trying to shoot a phantom. Shot after shot spewed from the gun but none of his bullets seemed capable of finding its target.

When the black stallion's front hoofs came thudding down on to the very rim of the canyon a cloud of debris was dislodged. It showered over the last of the Hortons. The gunman spun his mount violently away from the falling rocks.

When the dust cleared the horse and its master were gone.

Earl Horton shook his head and used

the back of his glove to wipe the dust from his eyes. Had he just imagined seeing the mysterious man whom he believed to be the legendary Skyhorse? He had just lost his only kin, and he wondered whether the shock had unhinged his mind.

Was he seeing things?

Could a heartless soul be affected by death when he had earned his blood money for so long dishing out nothing but death?

Horton snorted. He thrust the smoking .45 back into his holster and returned his thoughts to the wounded cowboy he and his brothers had been paid to kill. He gathered his reins up and looked beyond the fresh corpses to where the dense hoof dust filled the canyon. He could no longer see the beasts that had brutishly destroyed his younger brother, but he could still hear them as they charged further and further away from the bloody mayhem they had created.

The famed Lazy B longhorns were

between himself and the man he had been hired to kill, but they would not stop him achieving his goal. He would shoot every steer to get to the fleeing cowboy. Horton intended to honour the deal he had made with Solomon Casey.

He intended killing Appaloosa King.

The last of the Hortons gave out an insane scream, rammed his spurs into the flanks of his horse and thundered after the wounded cowboy.

15

The deadly hired gun had ridden along
the canyon until the sun had risen once
again. The bone-chilling cold of night
was replaced by the merciless rays that
grew hotter the higher the sun rose in
the blue, cloudless sky. Yet no matter
how far he rode Horton still could not
see the cowboy he sought.

The canyon was wider now and in
parts its once high walls had eroded
and collapsed. Horton had passed the
steers more than hour earlier and knew
that there was nothing between himself
and Appaloosa King. The stallion
beneath him started to slow as the hired
killer approached a wide stretch of
fast-flowing water.

Earl Horton drew rein and allowed
his horse to drink. He stared out ahead
of him, but apart from purple mesas far
off in the distance he could make

nothing out clearly. The frost on the ground had started to evaporate as soon as the sun had risen. Now a noisome heat haze surrounded him.

He knew the wounded cowboy must be somewhere ahead of him, but had no idea where. Horton threw one leg over his cantle and dropped to the ground. He held on to his reins as his lathered-up mount continued to drink. He studied the sun-baked ground; then he saw what he had been searching for.

Blood.

It was the blood of Appaloosa King.

The weary gunman knelt and looked at the droplets of crimson gore. There was a trail of it leading from the canyon behind him straight into the crystal-clear water.

Slowly Earl Horton rose back to his full height and rubbed his sleeve across his sweating brow. He pulled out his silver cigar case and opened it. He removed the last of the fat cigars from it, then returned the empty case back into his coat pocket.

He bit off the end of the cigar, then spat it at the trail of blood at his boots. He struck a match and cupped its flame to the cigar between his teeth. As smoke trailed from his mouth he nodded.

'Nobody can lose that much blood and live too long,' Horton mumbled.

The lethal avenger grabbed the saddle horn and eased himself up on to the saddle. He raised himself and balanced in his stirrups. His cruel eyes surveyed the land far ahead of him. Even the shimmering heat haze could not disguise the distant town of Deadlock. He lowered himself down again and pulled the horse's head up from the water.

'Whatever the name of that town is yonder, it looks like Appaloosa is headed for it,' Horton said to himself through a cloud of cigar smoke. 'I reckon he's thinking somebody there might save his bacon. I'm gonna prove him wrong.'

Earl Horton spurred and resumed his pursuit.

16

The blistering sun remained directly above the lone horseman as he drove his spurs into the flanks of the tall appaloosa stallion and wearily urged the sweat-covered animal ever onward. The cowboy was no coward but he instinctively knew that he was bleeding too freely to waste time in facing the bushwhacker. He had to get the wound sewn up to stop the flow of gore whilst there was still time. In all his days he had never treated any of his prized appaloosa horses the way he was treating the faithful stallion beneath his saddle.

But there was no choice.

He had to reach Deadlock and find a sawbones.

A man had only so much blood flowing through his veins and Appaloosa King knew he had spilled most of his. His trail gear was soaked in it, as was his saddle and horse. Time was running out and the cowboy was all too aware of that.

Through swirling skeins of moving haze the cowboy had caught glimpse of the distant settlement. Yet no matter how hard he spurred the trusty stallion he seemed to be unable to come any closer to it.

Clouds of mist filled his mind. They were something he had never experienced before. They mocked him as he fought against the pain and tried to keep his horse moving.

Dust kicked up from the hoofs of the galloping animal as it obeyed its master and continued to ride into the waves of humid heat that washed over it. The cowboy knew that by noon the heat haze tended to lift but it was still an awfully long way from noon and the rider doubted his chances of living that long.

Appaloosa King screwed up his eyes. There was nothing to see but the unyielding heat haze. He began to doubt whether he had actually seen the town at all. His mind was playing tricks on him and he did not understand how or why.

The valiant stallion was flagging beneath the rays of the unyielding sun. He had to allow the animal to rest, Appaloosa told himself. Even the best of horses could only run for so long before they dropped. The cowboy knew that Moon would keep going until its heart burst, but that was the last thing he wanted.

Defying his own agony, Appaloosa drew rein and dragged the stallion to an abrupt halt. The exhausted animal staggered as its master sat motionless for a few endless moments. Then the cowboy mustered up enough energy to raise his head. He looked all around him with blurred eyes. The horseman was confused as to whether he was actually surrounded by the morning heat haze or it was that his own eyes could no longer focus.

A pain tore through him. He lowered his head and at last admitted the agony that ravaged his tall, lean body. For a few moments he endured the pain, then somehow he managed to cast it off.

'It can't be far to Deadlock,' Appaloosa told himself over and over again. 'We gotta meet Miss Catherine off the train. I can't let her down. I can't let Judge Berkley down.'

He glanced down at the blood that covered his shirt front. The bullet which had hit him in the back hours before had gone clean through his body and exited just below his right collarbone. He teased the bloody fabric of his shirt away from his flesh and looked at the savage hole, which continued to bleed.

Appaloosa swung the high-shouldered mount round and gritted his teeth. He spat and ran a gloved hand along the neck of the distinctively marked stallion.

'You gotta get me to Deadlock, Moon boy,' the cowboy told the faithful horse. Somehow the horse had managed to keep going at pace long after most mounts would have pulled up lame. 'I have to get this wound tended whilst I still got some blood left.'

The stallion dragged a hoof across the dry sand as its master tried to see if he was still being chased. He raised a hand against the bright sun and squinted back. The stifling haze was thinner a few miles behind them but he still could not focus on anything clearly.

Then he saw something which troubled him. There was the shadow of a horse and rider in the depths of the mist. It was following the trail of bloody droplets he had left in his wake.

'Is that a rider?' Appaloosa no longer believed his dust-caked eyes. The heat haze danced before him, making the vague image appear and then vanish with each beat of his pounding heart. 'Could that be one of the critters who shot me? It could be a vulture. Damned if I can tell.'

The cowboy had begun to doubt his

tired mind. Nothing was the way he was used to. It was as if something was playing tricks with him, and that troubled the normally confident cowboy. He eased the horse round, then heard the distinctive sound of yet another horse to his right. Appaloosa was confused but still capable of knowing that it must be a different horse that he could hear off in the distance.

'Two of them, huh?' the cowboy reasoned as he managed to claw back a few scraps of his memory. 'Yeah, that's right. There were two of them back at the canyon. Reckon they've split up.'

Nothing made any sense to the cowboy any longer. A simple telegraph had led him into a cauldron of deadly lead. He tried to gather what was left of his wits and find an answer as to why he had been bushwhacked.

'I wonder who shot me?' Appaloosa muttered, fighting against the delirium that filled his mind with terrifying fog. Then another more troubling thought occurred to him. 'I wonder what happened to Billy and Dobie? I was sure that they'd have caught up with me by now.'

He had only just spoken when the answer to his question dawned on him.

'They would have caught up with me by now,' Appaloosa sighed heavily, 'if they were still alive.'

The young cowboy took hold of his horse's mane and eased its head in the direction he knew ought to lead to the distant town to which he was meant to have ridden to greet Judge Berkley's daughter when she arrived on the train.

He patted the stallion's neck.

'I really ought to get off your back and let you rest, Moon. Trouble is I got me a feeling that if I do I sure ain't gonna be able to climb back in the saddle.'

The stallion snorted as if it understood the words of its severely wounded master.

The land ahead of the wounded cowboy was in total contrast to the land known as the Lazy B. It was nothing but sand and sagebrush: a prairie littered with the bones of men and animals alike. This was quite unlike the terrain south of Sidewinder Canyon. That was a fertile land and this was a place that took no prisoners. It punished the weak or the unprepared. Just now Appaloosa felt as though he was both.

His mount required grain and water and he was shy of both.

Appaloosa blinked hard, but his eyes no longer obeyed. All he could see were blurred images. He lifted his canteen and shook it. It was barely a quarter full. He unscrewed its stopper and lifted it up with both hands to his lips. He managed to drink enough to quench his thirst. He then poured some of the precious liquid into the palm of his glove. He rubbed the water into his face.

'I sure hope I'm close to Deadlock.' Appaloosa tried to screw the stopper back on to the neck of the canteen but failed. It fell to the sand. Appaloosa poured the remainder of the water over his mount's head, then tossed the empty canteen away. Pain ripped through him again. It was like having a branding-iron pressed upon his flesh.

Appaloosa King hung over his saddle horn and watched his blood dripping on to his saddle rope. He steadied the tall stallion and tried to think, but he had lost far too much precious blood to be able to do so.

He blinked hard again. It made no difference.

The swirling heat haze that surrounded him and his proud mount grew no less frustrating to his tired eyes. He could see little further than ten feet away from where the appaloosa stood.

The cowboy then remembered the shot that had hit him in his back. He recalled little else after that, apart from being almost knocked from his saddle when the bullet had torn through him.

He shuddered. 'Gotta try and stop the bleeding.'

The cowboy tore his bandanna from his sweat-soaked neck and rammed its tail into the brutal bullet hole in his chest in an attempt to stem the flow of blood. He knew that the hole in his back was probably still losing blood but there was no way of reaching that.

The stallion looked back and pricked its ears as it stared into the heat haze. Its hoof pawed at the ground like a defiant bull daring the unseen rider to attack. Appaloosa knew that his mount had heard something.

Was it the same man who had shot him? It must be. He then thought about the other horseman he had heard moments before to his right.

'Reckon they're figuring on finishing the job they started, Moon boy,' Appaloosa murmured with a sigh. 'We have to get out of here real fast.'

The cowboy listened hard. He could hear the horse behind him approaching at speed. Whoever they were, they were coming at a pace far faster than most experienced riders would ever press their horses in this heat, his fog-filled mind told King. It could not be either of his pals.

Billy and Dobie would never force their mounts to build up a sweat in the prairie. They knew better. It must be the back-shooter.

If it was the same varmint who had shot him back at Sidewinder Canyon he would start shooting as soon as he caught sight of the distinctive stallion with the spotted rump, the cowboy wearily thought.

Appaloosa summoned every scrap of his dwindling strength and turned the high-shouldered horse around. Somewhere out there in the heat haze there was the town of Deadlock, the cowboy kept telling himself.

All he had to do was find it. Normally the skilled horseman could do that blindfolded. It was a whole lot harder to do anything when you had a bullet hole in your chest.

Even staying alive was becoming a real chore.

The horse shook its head and snorted. It was ready even if its master was not.

'Easy, Moon.' Appaloosa was panting like a hound dog as he fought to remain conscious. 'I gotta make sure I don't fall from this damn saddle.'

He lifted his cutting rope, looped it around his waist and secured it round the saddle horn. He cut the slack with his pocket knife, then nodded.

'That ought to do it.' The cowboy sighed. 'Now I can't fall even if I quit living.'

Appaloosa then concentrated on his boots as they kept him balanced in their tapadero-covered stirrups. It took every ounce of his dwindling strength just to remain awake. Just to keep his eyes open was a monumental feat.

He returned his hands to the reins and gathered them in. The rope ought to help him remain astride the stallion, he kept telling himself. He forced his pain-racked body to go rigid in an attempt to remain astride the tall stallion.

Even half-conscious the cowboy knew that the prairie was no place to fall from a horse if you wanted to survive. This was a merciless place; it took no prisoners.

Things died here.

Appaloosa did not want to become just another pile of bleached white bones. Again he thought about the judge's daughter and wondered what she looked like. He tried to keep that thought in his fog-filled mind.

'I ain't dying until I see her face,' he muttered. 'I sure hope she's real pretty.'

He inhaled as deeply as he could manage, then spurred.

The stallion responded as best it could. Yet even the most powerful of horses was labouring in the soft sand beneath its hoofs.

The magnificent appaloosa had barely managed to get into its stride before the chilling sound of a rifle being fired shook the humid air. Then another shot rang out.

This time Appaloosa felt the heat of the bullet as it passed within inches of his shoulder. Somehow the cowboy managed to turn in his saddle and look back through the rising hoof dust as Earl Horton rode out of the swirling heat haze.

The bright sunlight reflected off the unusual weapon in his gloved hands.

There was no mistaking the silver Winchester being cocked by the lethal hired gunman.

Appaloosa watched in horror as a spiral of smoke rose from the barrel of the rifle. Within a mere second another deadly bullet tore past the cowboy's flagging mount.

Even delirious, the cowboy knew that his attacker would not miss again. Appaloosa violently hauled his reins abruptly to his left. The stallion beneath him fell heavily into the soft sand.

The cowboy lay with one leg trapped beneath the hefty flank of the horse and battled to free himself of the rope that he had used to secure himself atop the stallion. As his hands fumbled for his knife Appaloosa could hear the rider coming closer and closer behind him.

The cowboy slid the honed blade of his knife through the restraints. Then he saw the dark shadow of the horseman spread over the sand.

Appaloosa tried to turn to see who was holding the silver rifle, but it was impossible. The winded stallion could not move and the cowboy's leg was still trapped between the saddle and the ground.

'Who are you?' Appaloosa managed to shout.

'Who am I? Hell, I'm your executioner, Appaloosa,' Earl Horton snarled down through the hazy air at his helpless victim.

The cowboy watched the shadow even though he could not see Horton directly. He saw the dark image of the rifleman dismounting with his rifle held high in his left hand.

'What's your name and why are you hunting me?' Appaloosa asked wearily as he vainly tried to free his trapped leg.

Earl Horton strode around the fallen stallion and trained the barrel of the Winchester on the helpless cowboy.

'The name's Horton.'

Appaloosa shook his head. It meant nothing to him. 'I've never heard of you.'

The hired killer stepped closer and cranked the hand guard of his rifle. He levelled the weapon at the foreman of the Lazy B. Horton was shaking. He wanted to kill the cowboy more than he had ever wanted to kill anyone.

'Think back. You stopped me and my brothers from collecting a real big wage a few years back,' the gunman railed.

Appaloosa looked at the man. The sun gleamed brightly off his rifle. 'I recall. Where are your brothers?'

'Dead,' Horton snorted. 'Back there in the canyon. Luke got himself bit by a sidewinder and Will was trampled to death by that damn herd of longhorns you stampeded.'

'I got me a feeling you'll be joining them when my pals show up, Horton,' the cowboy replied. 'It's only a matter . . . '

For a moment Appaloosa did not have the strength to finish his sentence.

'They're dead as well,' Earl Horton said. He smiled. 'I shot them the same way I shot you.'

The injured cowboy frowned sadly. 'Back-shot?'

'Yep.' Horton raised the rifle and aimed at his victim's skull. 'I'll finish you off nice and clean.'

'So all this killing is just revenge, huh?' the cowboy asked sadly. 'An eye for an eye.'

Horton shook his head. 'I don't kill unless somebody pays me to do so, Appaloosa. Me and my brothers were paid a mighty handsome sum to kill you.'

The cowboy was utterly confused. 'Who'd pay you to kill me?'

'A gent named Solomon Casey.'

Horton curled his finger around his rifle's trigger and aimed at the startled face of the cowboy. 'Now say your prayers.'

The deafening sound of rifle fire rang out across the prairie. The air vibrated. Then Earl Horton fell on to his back. A neat bullet hole in his chest was the only evidence that he was dead.

Then another long shadow stretched across the sand as a second horseman rode up to the body of the hired assassin. The stunned cowboy looked up at the strange figure upon the black stallion with the silver mane and tail.

'Who are you?' Appaloosa gasped. He watched the rider slide his smoking rifle back into its scabbard. 'I know we ain't ever met before but you sure look familiar.'

'They call me Skyhorse,' the horseman replied. 'Joe Skyhorse.'

'Why'd you save my bacon, Joe?' Appaloosa could feel his head spinning. 'Don't get me wrong, I'm mighty obliged.'

163

Skyhorse did not answer. There was no time. He could see that the injured cowboy was in far worse condition than he had at first supposed. He threw his leg over the stallion's silver mane and dropped to the ground. He moved quickly to Appaloosa and knelt. Just as his knee touched the ground the Lazy B foreman's head slumped down upon the sand.

Appaloosa King was falling helplessly into a dark abyss. It was an unholy place where nightmares were rife. He had never been there before.

Finale

The locomotive moved slowly into the cattle town of Deadlock like a great iron monster in search of fresh prey. Fiery sparks rose from its stack and mingled with the black, billowing smoke. It was late afternoon and the sun still had a couple of hours remaining before it sank below the horizon.

As the mighty engine hissed and slowed it drew the attention of the two watching men seated on the boardwalk just outside Doc Parry's ramshackle clinic. Both men were holding the reins of their lathered-up mounts.

'The doc did a good job patching you up, Appaloosa,' Skyhorse remarked.

The cowboy nodded his head. 'That's a fact, Joe. Wish I didn't have to wear this damn sling, though.'

'You must be mighty tough to have

survived losing so much blood,' Sky-horse went on.

'I'd not have survived at all if not for you.' Appaloosa patted the back of the man who had saved his life. 'What was in that drink you gave me out there on the prairie? I never tasted anything like it before. It sure bucked me up.'

Skyhorse shrugged. 'I ain't sure. A Cheyenne medicine man gave it to me. Whatever it was it brought you out of that deep sleep.'

Appaloosa stood when he saw the train come to a stop. He watched as porters jumped down and placed wooden steps on the ground. The handful of passengers began to disembark. The cowboy studied every one of them.

'Who you looking for?' Skyhorse asked.

Before the Lazy B foreman could reply he saw a beautiful young woman accept the hand of a porter and gracefully step down to the dusty ground.

'Her,' Appaloosa drawled.

He was like a moth being drawn to a

naked flame. He led his horse across the wide street towards the most beautiful creature he had ever set eyes upon.

'Miss Catherine?'

She looked at the cowboy before her. She was not repelled by his blood-stained trail gear. She looked into his face and saw something that made her step forwards.

'Do you work for my father?'

He nodded. 'I sure do. My name's Appaloosa. Judge Berkley sent me and a couple of boys to bring you home.'

She looked all around before her handsome eyes came back to his. There was concern in her expression.

'But you're alone, Appaloosa,' Catherine said. 'By the look of you I take it there was trouble on your journey here. Was there?'

'Yep, there was a whole heap of trouble and my pals were killed, ma'am.' The cowboy sighed sadly. Then he pointed at the porch of the doctor's clinic. 'If it weren't for that good-looking young man sitting over there with the black horse

I'd have been killed myself. He saved my bacon and brought me to town so I could get fixed up.'

Catherine moved to one side and looked at the doctor's clinic. Then she returned her attention to the cowboy. She was puzzled.

'What man? There's nobody there.'

'Don't you see him? He's sitting down. His horse is black as night and has a silver mane and tail, Miss Catherine.' Appaloosa turned and stared across the street. She was correct. There was no one there. His eyes searched the street but there was no sign of either the unusual horse or its master. The baffled cowboy turned back and faced the beautiful young woman. 'That's odd. Where'd he go?'

Catherine tilted her head and smiled at him. 'Are you OK, Appaloosa? You look as though you've just seen a ghost.'

The cowboy shook his head. A smile came to his face.

'I've got me a feeling that maybe I did, ma'am.'